CW01271816

THE BREAKING OF
THE SHELL

Hanneke Coates

authorHOUSE

AuthorHouse™ UK
1663 Liberty Drive
Bloomington, IN 47403 USA
www.authorhouse.co.uk
Phone: 0800.197.4150

© 2018 Hanneke Coates. All rights reserved.

No part of this book may be reproduced, stored in a retrieval system, or transmitted by any means without the written permission of the author.

Scripture quotations marked NIV are taken from the Holy Bible, New International Version®. NIV®. Copyright © 1973, 1978, 1984 by International Bible Society. Used by permission of Zondervan. All rights reserved. [Biblica]

Published by AuthorHouse 02/09/2018

ISBN: 978-1-5462-8734-6 (sc)
ISBN: 978-1-5462-8733-9 (e)

Print information available on the last page.

Any people depicted in stock imagery provided by Thinkstock are models, and such images are being used for illustrative purposes only.
Certain stock imagery © Thinkstock.

This book is printed on acid-free paper.

Because of the dynamic nature of the Internet, any web addresses or links contained in this book may have changed since publication and may no longer be valid. The views expressed in this work are solely those of the author and do not necessarily reflect the views of the publisher, and the publisher hereby disclaims any responsibility for them.

This story is dedicated to my dear mother,

Johanna Albertha Hoorn-Aergelo
1912–1996

While so many children died in the concentration camps,
my mother went in with two children
and three and a half years later came out with three.
Her courage and love were unsurpassed.

The Breaking of the Shell

This is a story of forgiveness and of the long painful journey it took to finally make my peace with those who have abused me.

In sharing this story, I pray that readers will be encouraged to take a first step towards the peace that awaits us when we believe in the power of reconciliation and forgiveness. This is a great prize.

We feel pain when God starts breaking the shells we wear around ourselves.

It is in Christ that we find out who we are and what we are living for. Long before we first heard of Christ, He had his eye on us, had designs on us for glorious living, part of the overall purpose he is working out in everything and everyone.

The Breaking of the Shell

And a woman spoke, saying, "Tell us of pain."

And he said:

Your pain is the breaking of the shell that encloses your understanding.

Even as the stone of the fruit must break, that its heart may stand in the sun, so you must know pain.

And could you keep your heart in wonder at the daily miracles of your life, your pain would not seem less wondrous than your joy;

And would you accept the seasons of your heart, even as you have always accepted the seasons that pass over your fields.

And would you watch with serenity through the winters of your grief.

Much of your pain is self-chosen.

It is the bitter potion by which the physician within you heals your sick self.

Therefore trust the physician, and drink his remedy in silence and tranquility.

For his hand, though heavy and hard, is guided by the tender hand of the Unseen,

And the cup he brings, though it burn your lips, has been fashioned of the clay which the Potter has moistened with His own sacred tears.

—Kahlil Gibran

Foreword

As founder of The Forgiveness Project I have witnessed many survivors of violence embark on a path towards understanding and even forgiveness. Some have been victim to a single brutal act, while others - like Hanneke Coates - have endured years of humiliation and torture. Yet all have come to understand that the after-shock of trauma can reverberate across the generations and down the years if meaning is not found through healing, restoration and forgiveness.

Hanneke is one of The Forgiveness Project storytellers, or you could call her a *story healer* because over the past ten years she has told her story in many schools and church halls giving hope and encouragement to those who cannot move beyond their pain. Healing comes from finding the gift in the wound – in Hanneke's case a determination not to let the future be driven by the sins of the past.

The Breaking of the Shell is a remarkable memoir of a story not yet told, beginning with the invasion of Java by the Japanese in 1942 when as a small child Hanneke becomes a prisoner in one of the 300 concentration camps based around the archipelago. Here we are introduced to a world of unremitting cruelty and injustice where the strategy of the Japanese guards is to annihilate their Dutch prisoners through neglect and slow starvation. The scars of sadistic punishment and ritual humiliation are etched deep in the young Hanneke, leading in adulthood to an abusive marriage and deep feelings of worthlessness.

The Breaking of the Shell powerfully depicts how people become cold-blooded killers by a process of dehumanising their victims. Many similar examples exist, for instance in Gitta Sereny's interviews with the SS commandant Franz Stangl where he refers to his victims as cargo rather than human beings; when Sereny asked him whether seeing children lined up for the gas chambers made him think of his own children, he replied: "I rarely saw them as individuals. It was always a huge mass... they were naked, packed together, running, being driven with whips..." During the Holocaust, Nazis referred to Jews as rats in the same way that Hutus in the Rwanda genocide called Tutsis cockroaches. Hanneke's Camp Commander makes his Dutch captives jump around on all fours and croak like frogs.

Any of us who attempt to understand evil may be accused of forgiving the unforgiveable. However, the struggle is not with condoning but with empathising while maintaining moral integrity. Hanneke does not empathize with her cruel captors as such but she does set out a picture where you can't help but wonder…. given similar conditions which of us might be capable of such extreme cruelty?

For Hanneke healing is gradual, found in the 'storms of life' and manifesting in the form of forgiveness. But this is not forgiveness conditional on remorse or apology, but rather forgiveness as an act of self-healing – an acceptance that evil is a uniquely human feature and we cannot let its aftershocks taint or destroy us. Here too perhaps is an understanding that the hate which had shattered her life must end with her. Forgiveness thus becomes a final liberation. In later years too Hanneke is finally able to find respect and compassion for the Japanese people who she had come to fear and distrust. Indeed, she pays tribute to some remarkable Japanese individuals who today go to extensive lengths to remember the camps and honour the victims.

Reading Hanneke's memoir you will come away with a deeper appreciation of the impossible and yet essential need for forgiveness in a historical conflict where truth and facts have taken decades to emerge. Breaking the cycle of trauma is about breaking the cycle of silence and in the telling of what happened Hanneke has been both transcending and transforming her own story.

This is a book that sets out to examine issues of freedom, responsibility and reconciliation. Hanneke's return to Japan decades later and the subsequent work she has done to promote peace and understanding round the world, is an example of reconciliation in action. As with other stories that I've collected over the years, her story not only embodies a model for repairing broken hearts but can also shed light on our own smaller grievances and provide fresh perspectives. As a reader you are left with a strong sense that if we are ever to move beyond the pain of the past it must be the responsibility of the living to heal the dead.

Marina Cantacuzino
Founder of The Forgiveness Project

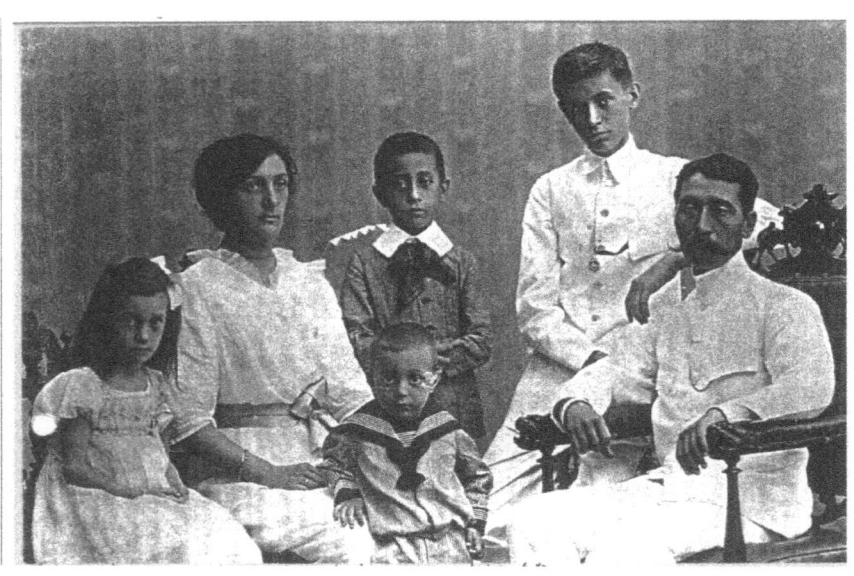

My Grandparents - This picture was probably taken around 1914
(Mary, Koos, Adrie, Eddy, Niek and Franciscus)

Our very first picture taken to send to Holland
(Balikpapan 1946)

Nicolette on the left and Hanneke on the right (Hanneke's first doll, Loesje that has arrived from Holland)

These pictures were taken in Holland (the picture on the left were Heleen , Frank, Hanneke and Nicolette and the picture on the right is Hanneke with Red Cross outfit and her beloved doll Loesje)

Niek e Jo Hoorn - Aergelo (Surabaya Java 1955)

IMPERIAL JAPANESE ARMY

Date 10-6-44

Your mails (and ~~~~~~~) a~ received ~~with thanks.~~
My health is (good, usual, ~~poor~~)
~~I am ill in hospital.~~
I am working for pay (~~I am paid~~ monthly salary).
~~I am not working.~~
My best regards to JO AND KINDEREN

Yours ever,

FROM:
Name. J.N. HOORN
Nationality. DUTCH
Rank. Sgt
Camp. P.O.W. OSAKA

To: MRS J.N. HOORN
NASSAULAAN 32
BANDOENG. JAVA

QQ 14.688

Orchideen Laan 17 ←
Bandoeng
Camp Tjihappit

← Our camp number

1947 . Our first passport photograph from LTR (Hanneke, Frank, Heleen, Nicolette and Mammie at the back)

Niek in the KNIL 1934
Midden voor Tjimahi

Tjihapit Java, 1944

I am sitting on the top step of a *stoepje*. It is early in the morning, and the mist is slowly rising and lifting away from the bungalows around us and floating around the surrounding volcanic mountains of the Bandoeng highlands. I watch the mist dissolve into nothing, where sun and earth greet each other at the start of a new day.

To my left, a small procession of women approach on the dusty path between the houses. They are all emaciated, all wearing shorts and bras made from faded cotton prints. They carry between them a small sausage-shaped burden of *tikar* matting. The sausage is handled lovingly and with infinite care. I can smell the matting.

Nothing in the world smells like this matting. Most of us sleep on our own bit of matting. Some are lucky and sleep on mattresses, but I sleep on tikar, so I know its smell intimately. It is a smell that goes back to my early childhood.

I also know why the women carry the sausage with such reverence. They do not cry or weep. There is a great sense of dignity, togetherness, and resignation. Two women gently drape their arms around the woman I know as Tante Lies. They carry a spade each. I know where they are going. They will carry the sausage as far as the gates of the camp.

Two Japanese soldiers stand by the gates, their bayonet rifles at ease between their booted legs. They wear khaki uniforms and shiny, polished boots, and in the tops of their boots I can see the tops of their whips. All soldiers carry whips in the sides of their boots. I know all about their whips …

The women stop in front of the soldiers and bow deeply, but not before they have looked straight into the Japanese soldiers' eyes. The women always look the soldiers straight in the eyes. There is a pride and defiance in their look, and the soldiers do not like it.

The women stand patiently, deeply bowed, till they are given the signal to move through the gate. The little sausage rests gently on the dusty road, but the women keep hold of it.

OK, OK, growls the Japanese soldier, and the women lift their heads and their little burden and again meet the soldier's eyes briefly before they continue their sorrowful way. They walk slowly for another five minutes on a narrow path that takes them into the jungle, till they come into a clearing. There are many little hillocks, some with crosses crudely made from sticks, some bare of any adornment, some with green blankets of new little grass blades peeping through the red ochre soil.

The two women carrying the little bundle gently put it down, while the spade-carrying women start digging a hole. It takes a long time, and they take turns digging and resting. But not Tante Lies. She just sits with the little sausage at her feet. There are no tears.

The women come here often.

Only a few days ago, my little friend Robbie and I were playing together. Life is here one day and gone the next. It takes very little to die in our camps, as there is almost no food or medication. The young and old go quickly.

There are no toys for us to play with, and school is not allowed by the Nippon, but we do play with sticks and stones, and we know numerous songs. We have known no different in our short lives.

We are confronted with death all the time, and many of my little friends have died of malaria, malnutrition, beriberi, or dysentery. Many of the aunties have died too, but we know no better.

Robbie will play no longer, and it will not take very long for the jungle to cover his little hillock. There will be nothing visible to remind us of little Robbie, but we will remember him in our hearts.

Tjihapit, 1944

The Bandoeng Camp is called Tjihapit. It lies in the mountainous region of mid Java, twenty-three hundred metres above sea level.

Lofty peaks and mighty active volcanos, where sulphurous fumes swirl up the verdant slopes, surround this cool town with its wide boulevards, colonial homes, and tree-lined roads. The street we live in is called Orchideen Straat; it is not far from the parade ground and the edge of the camp. A small concrete bridge crosses over the deep ditch that carries the monsoon waters, as well as the sewerage produced by each household, from the garden to the unmetalled road.

The bungalow has three bedrooms as well as the usual other rooms and servants' quarters. We live in this small bungalow together with almost a hundred other women and children. We are each allocated just forty-five centimetres of sleeping space.

The street is lined with purple flowering jacaranda trees. The fallen blossoms provide an endless source of play material for a small girl.

Six thousand women and children are incarcerated in small fenced-in sections of this once wealthy town. Another six thousand are in the other Bandoeng Camp, Karees.

The hot weather gives me prickly heat, and I am always scratching the itchy places. The sores round my legs and behind my ears are bothering me. By nightfall the little blisters have gone septic. There are no medications in the camp, and the rumour is that any Red Cross parcels containing badly needed medicine that do reach the camps are being swiped by the Nippon. (After the war the rumours are proven right, when sheds full of unopened Red Cross parcels are found.)

Mammie gets very cross when she finds me scratching away. 'Han, leave it alone!' She tells me to lick it, and indeed, it does relieve the itching.

Cholera, beriberi, malaria, dysentery (both amoebic and bacterial), and tropical ulcers are rife; we all suffer from these tropical diseases. The women and children succumb quickly to these dreadful diseases, mainly on account of our general malnutrition and weakness.

Mammie has been taken away on a stretcher. Only the very ill go into the hospital, and more often than not they will not be seen again. Mammie's legs are so swollen and puffy with beriberi that she can no longer work, or walk, or care for us.

In later years she will tell us that she was taken to Boemi Kamp, or Ziekenzorg (hospital care). For a very long time not one of our house companions knew where she had been taken. The long and arduous trip to Boemi on a stretcher left her almost dead, and she recalled lying on the Bandoeng station platform, waiting to be moved, and thinking quite philosophically that she would never see her children again but feeling too sick and tired to care a great deal.

The other women sharing our house collectively take over caring for us. Three extra small children cannot be easy, but the 'aunties' do not think twice about this act of mercy. There is no knowing when, or indeed if, our mother will ever return. Many months later and quite by chance, someone from the Solo Camp in Boemi reports having seen our mother there.

Boemi houses four thousand sick women and children, with only three doctors caring for them and almost no medication. But the nuns and young Australian nurses used in the hospital provide plenty of TLC.

It is a miracle that we are eventually reunited. Without the selfless care of the other women, many of us children would not have survived. The Dutch women were made of stern stuff. Stoic, down to earth, unsentimental, and tough to the bone they were—all qualities for survival.

The care of children in the women's camps was the antidote for apathy, too. The women became tigresses defending their young, fearless of the might of the Nippon.

After the war, it was found that the men's camps had suffered far greater losses, not because their treatment had been any worse than ours, but because psychologically they had not stood up to the cruelty of the Japs. They'd had nothing to fight for, unlike the women.

> Now my heart is troubled and what shall I
> say? Father save me from this hour?
> No it was for this very reason I came to this hour
>
> —John 12:27 NIV

Suffering either gives me myself or it destroys me.
The way to find self is in the fires of sorrow.
If you find yourself in the fires of sorrow, God makes you nourishment for other people.

Laan Trivelli

TJIDENG WEST JAVA, 1944

Tjideng is the name of our final camp; it is part of the capital of Java Batavia (now Jakarta). Tjideng lies south-west of Tantjoengpriok Batavia's harbour and east of the railway line. We have come here by train from Bandoeng, hundreds of woman and children packed tightly in cattle-truck trains.

Ironically, it was my maternal great-grandfather who was summoned by 'royal command' to sail to the Dutch East Indies and supervise the building of this line right through the jungle and mangroves to make East and West Java more accessible.

There are no windows or any facilities for us. Denied food or drink or seating, many people have died on these journeys. The very old and the very young are always the first victims.

With her three small children, already undernourished for some years, my mother struggles to keep from succumbing to despair in this stinking, airless, locked-up deathtrap. The responsibility of taking care of us alone for so long must weigh heavily on her.

Normally this journey would have taken just hours, but the bureaucratic Nippon system has managed to stretch it to days. Stopping and starting, leaving the long train standing in the hot tropical sun, and shunting into side tracks for hours on end has stretched the survival instinct of those inside to their limits.

Tjideng, in contrast to the cool mountains of mid Java's Bandoeng, is hot and humid. It lies on the western side of Batavia, the Tjideng River to one side, the Banjir canal (flood canal) on another, with the railway line completing the triangle. A bamboo fence known as *gedekking*, topped and reinforced by barbed wire and patrolled day and night by armed Nippons, encloses the camp.

There may be 10,500 woman and children in our camp, all packed into the 220 houses round Tjideng. More arrive daily, packing us more tightly, depriving us of more food with every new contingent.

Young boys of 10 or 11, depending on how tall they have grown, are taken away from their mothers and sent to the men's camps, where slave labour awaits them. We live with many, many other women and children in a house in *Laan Trivelli* (Trivelli Lane). Small children sleep like sardines in a tin, head to toe.

The other facilities come under increasing pressure also. There is no electricity. One tap with no more than a trickle of water coming from it has to provide drinking, cooking, bathing, and washing water for more than a hundred housemates.

Many hours of our days and nights are filled by standing and bowing to attention while facing the 'circle of the sun' Japanese flag on the parade ground. Thus leisure time for performing ablutions is limited, putting more pressure on the sharing of facilities.

We are, however, the lucky ones who have the whole bathroom-turned-into-sleeping-quarters to ourselves. The other house occupants are worried about the noise three small children can make, and so we have a measure of rare privacy in these cramped conditions.

Laan Trivelli is not far from the main camp gates. My big sister, Nicolette, and I wander down there to see the two caged monkeys that belong to the camp commander, Sonei.

Mammie tells us never to go close. The poor caged creatures are vicious, and they bite. They curl their lips when they see us approach, showing their yellow teeth. There is a delicious sense of fear inside me, together with a mixture of sadness and curiosity, but Nicolette will have none of it. She pulls at my hand when I want to get closer. '*Pas op*, Han!' says Nicolette—be careful!—' They will bite you if you go any closer."

We are both mesmerized by the piles of fruit lying on the floor of the cage. We are always hungry, and it is strangely satisfying to feast our eyes on the abundance of half-consumed fruit. The monkeys are called Nelly and Kees—a strange choice of Dutch names for a pair of Nippon monkeys.

When there is a full moon, our camp commander goes into his moon-mad phase. He opens the cage and allows the monkeys to go free and terrorize the camp population. They go on the rampage, screaming and showing their yellow fangs. They climb in and under and over everything, biting children and adults alike. Even the Nippon soldiers run screaming out of their path.

In the tropics a wound or scratch or a simple mosquito bite can go septic in just a few hours. A monkey bite may mean the end of your days.

Our little brother, Frank, is born in the camp Tjihapit, at the Roman Catholic Hospital, Boromeus. He is named Frank, as this means 'freedom'. We almost did not have a brother. Shortly before he was born, my Pappie came to the camp fencing to say goodbye to us before being transported to work on the Burma Railway. It was difficult to have a conversation across the gedekking, so he pointed at Mammie's big pregnant tummy, mouthing, 'How much longer?' In reply she held up two fingers to indicate two months. A Nippon standing close by saw two fingers being held up and took this to be the sign of victory. Quick as a flash he picked up a nearby brick and hurled it at my Mammie's tummy. There were many other women standing by the fence saying goodbye to departing husbands and sons. In an instant they moved in front of her, taking the brunt of the impact and shouting, 'Get away, get away!' to Mammie, saving the life of my brother.

Frank's hair is almost white, so the women affectionately call him Witkwast, the Dutch word for a soft brush to apply lime onto walls. Frank has only ever known camp life. Nicolette and I take care of him, while Mammie's job is to move furniture for the Nippon during the day. The furniture is stolen from the now-empty houses of the Europeans; it will eventually be shipped over to grace the homes of the Japanese higher-ranking army officers.

We have to grow up fast, and the responsibilities are big for such small people. Our senses are tuned sharp as we learn to survive in this hostile environment.

One day Nicolette hears Frank, who has learned to sit up in his cot, make a very strange noise. She is instantly alerted and goes to look for an adult. When Mammie comes to look, she finds Frank's little face puce—he is dangling from his mosquito net. She quickly releases Frank from the net and his little face soon returns to its natural colour.

This story is told and retold many times like a tale of great heroism.

There is no school, as the Nippon has forbidden any kind of teaching. In any case, there are no books or pens or paper. The women teach us songs and games when the coast is clear and no Nippon is in sight. There is great apathy among the older children, and the lack of education is deeply felt.

We *djonkok* (squat down as only children of the tropics can do for hours at the time) in the dusty sand and play with sticks and stones in our world of make-belief. Most games revolve round mealtimes, cooking scenes, tea parties, and so on—anything to do with food, as this is always at the forefront of our minds.

The women also spend a large part of the day discussing recipes, the more exotic the better. But for most of the time we sit around doing nothing, as we have little energy on the meagre rations the communal kitchens provide. For a long time now we have had only one meal per day, consisting of one cup of rice and one cup of water-lily soup.

Mammie has found a good trick of making the tiny portions of bread we sometimes get last longer. She dries the pieces in the sun till they are bone dry and rock hard.

We have to sit and watch and not let the bread out of sight during the drying process, as stealing is rife in the camp. When at last the crusts have gone crisp, we suck and suck with relish till the last crumbs have melted in our mouths. It takes an entire morning to dry and eat a crust.

Laan Trivelli is now known as Jl. Tanah Abang II. It can be found off Jl. Merdeka Barat at the National Monument Monas. This square used to be known as Konings Plein (Kings square).

The Kapok Tree

Often we are told by our captors that our country has behaved disgracefully towards our oppressor, which is quickly translated by the woman as most probably some military victory gained by our own soldiers.

Optimism is part of the survival skills practised by everyone. But today we are brought to the parade ground to be shown a sight we are unlikely to forget. Two Dutch soldiers have been caught making contact with their family through the gedekking perimeter. They have been made an example of to everyone.

Close to the gedekking stands a huge kapok tree. Its branches are horizontal and bare apart from the large pods of kapok dangling from their thin threads.

Halfway up the tree hang the two soldiers by their necks, gently swinging. I can see their khaki shorts are stained dark round the crotch from the dried faeces and urine. I can see their bloated faces and their ribs through the white skin. I can hear the steady buzz of the flies around the bodies. Every detail of this grizzly scene will be etched upon my mind for the rest of my life.

Every detail of the atmosphere will haunt me in my dreams. The softly weeping women. The undercurrent of raw anger. The disbelief at the injustice of it all. The sorrow at God's world gone mad. There is a curious mixture of private grief to each of us and the sense of corporate grieving that brings out defiance, toughness, protectiveness, and an iron will to survive whatever the Nippon do to us. We will not let them crack us, however much they humiliate.

In Romans 8:18 it says that our present sufferings are not worth comparing with the glory that will be revealed in us.

Affliction can be a means of refining and purification. Many a life has come forth from the furnace of affliction more beautiful and more useful.

Affliction may also be for our strengthening and development. And so we learn through the trials we are called upon to bear.

But how does it affect a small girl staring at the two khaki-clad men dangling from their tree?

There are some things in life that, humanly speaking, we may never come to terms with. It is seventy years later when I have finally learned to let go and let God take this part of my life and use it in the refining of my love for Him.

FORGIVENESS IS THE FRAGRANCE OF THE VIOLET THAT SHEDS ON THE HEEL THAT HAS CRUSHED IT.

—Mark Twain

Days Of Punishment

We have been called to *appel, tenko*, (appel is theDutch word for standing on parade Tenko is the English word for it. The BBC did a series on the camps which was called "TENKO) The Nippon are in a very angry mood. This is nothing new, as they are always ranting and raving. They are always angry about something. They shout and scream, and the person nearest to them can expect a beating around the head, a boot jerked violently in their direction, or a whip lashed around.

It does not really matter whether the nearest person is a child or adult, old or young; the Nippons will take out their anger and frustration on those within whipping distance. They scream their displeasure, they scream their commands, they scream all the time to humiliate.

We children are so terrified that we always do what is asked from us in an instant. In the short lives we have lived, we have been conditioned to be humiliated and never question or protest at whatever is asked from us.

When called to appel, tenko, we drop whatever we are doing, take Mammie's hand, and move to the parade ground as fast as our little legs will carry us.

There are four commands in Japanese that every child obeys.

Kiotské means 'stand to attention'. We stand in neat rows at a certain distance from each other. The rows must be separated widely enough for a whip-wielding Nippon to pass between. His shiny brown boots come striding towards us, and his shadow passes, while all the time the screaming continues.

Nové means 'stand upright', and we do stand ramrod, not moving a muscle.

Keré, the hardest of all, means 'bow'. We bow all day long. Each time a Jap comes into our field of vision, we bow and remain standing bowed till he is out of sight.

We stand bowing on the parade ground for many hours. Sometimes the heat is so severe that I lose track of anything going on around me, and I fall asleep standing up. Mammie and anyone else around me will catch, haul me up, and in a whisper tell me to keep awake. There is no space for gentleness or sympathy for a small girl who is tired out. The consequences are far too serious to allow softness on the parade ground.

We all suffer permanently from dysentery, and pools of faeces or urine are commonplace during lengthy punishments. Children and adults alike simply let it run.

Wakeré means 'stand at ease'.

Mostly we are not told what it is that has annoyed the Nippon sufficiently to bring thousands of women and children to the parade ground to be screamed at and humiliated for hours on end. Appel, tenko occupies a very large part of the Nippon's control over us.

Letting Go And Letting God

Some of the punishments meted out were almost always directed at all the inmates of the camps. Many punishments were sadistic and made doubly so by forcing old and young, sick or dying to stand on the parade ground and watch them being meted out in the heat of the noonday sun. Here are just a few of them.

1. The entire camp, including those from sickbay, had to remain in the bowing position in the heat of the day, under the relentless tropical sun at forty degrees Celsius, for up to three hours or more.
2. Punishment for *gedekking*. This was the buying of food illegally through the fence of bamboo matting. At the beginning of their internment at the camps, people still had money to buy food from the locals. Later on, jewellery, including wedding rings and other valuables were exchanged for tiny amounts of food. One banana, or an egg, often of dubious age, or red-hot chilies, were valuable sources of vitamins and much prized by the prisoners.

    The natives did a brisk trade with prisoners, but it was a very punishable offence if found out. Kneeling for many hours on the ground with a piece of sharp ended bamboo wedged between the lower leg and thigh. Even the smallest movement would wedge the sharp ends into the flesh. This was a favourite punishment inflicted, especially on young women, and watched by all the camp for extra effect.
3. Punishment of humiliation: hacking off all the hair with a very blunt pair of scissors or knife. Resulting in large chunks of scalp skin being torn off also.

    The way we were screamed at throughout the day and often at night, too.

4. Withholding of food. One, two, or even three days' supply would be withheld, according to the severity of the 'crime'. These punishments were always meted out to the entire camp.
5. Severe beatings or whipping. Every Jap officer carried a whip in the side of his tall leather boot.

All these punishments were carried out in full view of the entire assembled camp, for maximum humiliation.

I suppose as a surviving child of those camps, the deepest scars and the most lasting effects I have from those years are not from the lack of basic facilities, nor from witnessing the endless crimes inflicted on humanity. Neither did the pitiful state of my body leave a lasting effect, other than a dodgy and scoliotic spine.

It was the effect of the 'conditioning to be humiliated' that lasted longest. To be conditioned to be humiliated is to be in a state of spiritual poverty. It leaves a human being feeling worthless. It destroys all confidence and any acceptance of gifts we may possess. It also allows others to manipulate us into a need to be needed, a need to be loved.

It set me up to remain in a forty-year marriage in which I had become a victim of bullying, humiliation, and domestic violence, which finally dictated the breakup of it.

It left me forever searching for my true identity, never recognizing the simple fact that I am a child of God, that I was made in His own likeness and therefore am acceptable to God and loved by Him, just as I am.

IT IS OFTEN WHEN WE ARE AT THE DEPTH OF DESPAIR THAT WE CALL OUT TO GOD

It was LEON BLOY who wrote;
There are places in man's heart which do not yet exist and into them enters suffering, so that they may have existence

It is when we are suffering that we call out to God and only then do we begin to understand who we are and what resources there are within us. It was only when I learned to let go and let God that I began to realise that I was not a victim but a child of God, loved and accepted.

The love of reconciliation demands courage, strength, generosity of heart, patience, the wise art of peace, The living gently with our fellow travellers

Do not believe it offence against true justice or maybe denies the right of the poor who have suffered as a result of war crimes,

Annonymous

Frogs From Froggy Land

By 30 April 1945, the Allied American army had conquered the Japanese island of Okinawa, and on the same day Hitler had committed suicide in his secret and 'safe' bunker—bad news for the Japanese. As always, the Japanese would find some kind of punishment for all those incarcerated in the concentration camps.

Our own camp, Commander Sonei was especially good at finding the most humiliatingly cruel punishments for us. Thus we were commanded to stand on appèl, tenko that April day of 1945 in the burning tropical sun.

Sonei, the emperor's commander, sat atop a large white horse, his chest full of glittering medals and colourful ribbons, surveying the miserable mass of humiliated humanity.

Sonei carried his usual array of torture weapons. He had a gun, to shoot and kill, regardless of whether it was a child, a mother, old, or sick. His long whip would reach out to anyone, the whipping sound swishing in the hot air and making my skin ripple with terrified anticipation of being hit. Anyone suspected of breaking the rules, or of making the wrong movement by the tiniest of fractions, would be hit. There was also a thick, long bamboo stick, cut into a sharply pointed end, strong enough to kill, or take the skin off a body, or poke out an eye.

Sonei would not hesitate to inflict the most appalling injuries, which would turn septic in the filthy, hot environment of thousands of bodies, without much sanitation, packed together like sardines in a tin under the burning tropical sun.

There were about eleven thousand of us on the parade ground that day, and when Sonei thought he was tired of watching the thousands of women sweating like pigs, the children falling about from exhaustion and heat, and seeing the old and sick being supported and held up, he would think up a new game of torture.

Sonei ordered us to be what we were to the Japanese: we were the frogs from Froggy Land—the Dutch from Holland. So we were ordered to get on our haunches and jump about to honour the Japanese emperor. *Tenno Leika Banzai*—Hurray for the Emperor!

Slowly it dawned on the eleven thousand thin, starved, shaken, humiliated women and children that we were to start jumping around like frogs, crouching on all fours. This is hard enough when one is fit and healthy, but most of us had been through various appalling tropical diseases, not to mention three and a half years of starvation and shortage of water. Energy levels were below zero and the humiliation factor at its most brutal.

For an hour this entertained Sonei and his entourage of brown-khaki minions, while they whipped those who fell over from exhaustion. We were then ordered to croak—'Croak, you frogs from Froggy Land!'—and jump, and croak, again, and again. We croaked and jumped for several hours. Many of the old and young would die that day in humiliation and from torture, croaking and croaking and jumping.

Tenno Leika Banzai

Those of us who survived had our meagre ration of half a coconut filled with rice and some thin soup made from water lilies withheld for three days.

We had no food—just hunger, hunger, hunger. To be always hungry was very much part of our lives, and even today, seventy years later, I cannot waste even the smallest crust of bread.

We were indoctrinated to believe that all this suffering was in honour of the Japanese emperor: Tenno Leika Banzai—all to the honour of the emperor. We were frequently told that we should be thankful to be the guests of the emperor.

As a camp child, I learned very quickly to do what I was ordered to do. When we were called to Appèl to stand in the burning sun for many hours, to be counted and counted over and over again, I would instantly drop whatever I was doing and obey the screaming, yelling, whip-wielding soldier, find my mother and siblings, and stand to attention—or bow, or turn, or stand, or bow.

Hanneke Coates

PEACE IS THE FRUIT OF THE SPIRIT
BUT TO ACQUIRE IT
WE HAVE TO DO OUR PART,
WE HAVE TO TRANSFORM TORMENT, ANGUISH, INNER STRUGGLES
UNCERTAINTIES.
AND MOMENTS OF ARIDITY AND TEMPTATION
INTO OCCASIONS TO LOVE GOD

Tjideng Camp, The Bacon Row

It has become harder and harder to get food. We are all so thin that our ribs are prominent. Arms and legs are no more than sticks, and the children's eyes are huge in their sunken little faces. The women have not had periods for years, and young teenage girls that should have begun do not yet know what it is like to have them. It is nature's way of protecting their bodies from more losses. Their breasts are like little flat purses and are jokingly referred to as peas on a corrugated scrubbing board!

The Nippon policy of slow starvation and genocide of the European population in the Far East is now having a marked effect. Every day five or six people die, just in our immediate part of the camp. But it has not extinguished the sense of humour and fun these Dutch women have. It is their deep sense of camaraderie and community, their deep feeling of responsibility for each other, that keeps the survivors going.

As mentioned, the women are fiercely protective of their children. They have something to fight and live for; they are part of a community. Even in the hardest days of the war, amid child mortality, degradation, beatings, starvation, fear, and constant illness, there is one word that never crosses their lips: *doubt*. The women never doubt that victory will be theirs. Nippon will be defeated.

Not *all* the women care for their neighbours; there is the odd one who cares only for herself. She does not share but prefers to hoard. But it is not the few who cannot share and who display the less-human traits that stand out, it is the great majority who show just how exceptional the Dutch women are. They are strong, stoic, courageous, just, and long-suffering, but most of all they are original thinkers with a good dose of rebellion to stand up to the oppressor. They are never afraid to put their heads on the block for the good of the whole camp.

The woman who knew about the side of bacon had befriended the camp commandant, Morowi. He had rewarded her for a favour given to him, and she decided to keep the side of meat for herself.

Like all of us, she lives in a house packed full of other women. There is nowhere to hide meat without being found out. The others would smell it long before the aroma of cooking would give it away.

There is a permanent curfew after dusk, but her friendship with Morowi gives this woman the courage, when darkness has fallen, to bury the bacon in the bit of garden that belongs to the house she shares. Alas, a dog from a nearby *kampong* (village) finds his way into the camp, and his sensitive nose sniffs out the bacon, even in its underground hidey-hole.

With so many people around, nothing remains unseen for very long. The dog is caught and the precious bacon triumphantly rescued. The women immediately inform Morowi, who climbs on his motorcycle and at great speed arrives at the woman's house, where he confronts her.

No disturbance goes without punishment, and typically, not the guilty woman but the person nearest Morowi is beaten black and blue. Her hair is pulled, and she is whipped. The next day she will be humiliated in front of the whole camp by having her hair hacked off with a blunt knife, blunt enough to tear chunks off her scalp.

All of us are punished by more 'appel'. All the women and children, including those from sickbay, are left standing in neat rows, while bowing deeply for three or four or more hours, in temperatures of forty degrees Celsius. The guards walk between the rows, using their whips on anyone moving or trying to get more comfortable.

We three little ones surround Mammie, who is shaking with fear. I tell her that if she bows low enough the whip will not touch us when the Nippon swishes it across. A small smile appears on her face, and I beam with pleasure when she tells me what a clever girl I am.

When life is so devoid of excitement of any kind, the bacon-row story will be repeated many times to anyone wanting to share it.

In later life I have often wondered whether it was God's grace that kept us from falling over and whether this prepared me for other traumas experienced in later years. As children, we accept the circumstances in which we are brought up as normal. It has to follow that as adults we reap the rewards for having grown in that grace. We simply do not know any better and do not remember the luxuries from before that world.

There is always hope and trust in the adult's thoughts, but we trust and accept. Our trust in our mothers is deep-rooted and unconditional. We have no concept of what is normality. The most ordinary things are nothing more than fairy stories, as real as when my grandchildren wear make-believe crowns to be kings or queens in play.

We have been told about chocolate, but we have not an inkling of what it is. What is a teapot, or a bed? What is a fridge? What are clothes other than the rags we wear? What is lemonade, or milk, or vegetables?

We play make-believe, and I am the child, Nicolette the mammie, and Frank the pappie. Frank protests: 'I do not want to be Pappie today.'

Nicolette keeps us in order and questions Frank: 'Why do you not want to be the Pappie today?' Our father is no more than the top half of a man in a black-and-white photograph. The only other men we know about are the Japanese, and we have learned to fear them. They carry whips in the top of their boots. They scream their commands. Everything we have to do for them has the constant command *lekas, lekas!* tagged onto the order; that is Malay for 'quick, quick!' Everything has to be obeyed that instant.

Obeying The Nippon

When a Nippon comes into view, we have to drop whatever we are engaged in doing at once and bow deeply. Only when his back view is visible can we straighten out and continue whatever we are doing.

There are no vehicles in the camp save the odd motorcycle or Jap lorry. Our streets are empty of traffic. I am walking in the middle of the street on an errand to Tante Maud, when to my astonishment I spot a khaki-coloured lorry coming towards me, and suddenly I realize that the person at the steering wheel is a Nippon. Instantly I bow where I am rooted, in the middle of the street. I can hear the rumble of the engine coming closer and closer, but I must obey—I must obey, I must obey! Seconds before the lorry is upon me, a woman pulls me to safety.

I am acutely aware of being the cause of the furious shouting and yelling and fist-waving from the Nippon. His face, contorted in fury, is screaming a stream of abuse in Japanese, which I do not understand but know to be offensive.

We normally try to communicate in Malay with the Nippon, which we all speak fluently but the Nippon does not. There are few interpreters in the camps. In any case, generally speaking we do not speak to the Nippon; he speaks to us and barks his orders. Only those nominated as camp leaders may speak to them, but only then after having asked and been given permission to do so.

The camp leaders are leaders in every sense of the word. They show no fear but at the same time show courteous respect for the oppressor. Often they will be courageous enough to stand up and be counted if they know the Nippon has gone too far—many times with dire consequences. The Jap will think nothing of beating a woman to within an inch of her life. But just occasionally and inexplicably he will respond favourably, as in the case of the Bible Rebellion.

For I was hungry and you gave me something to eat,
I was thirsty and you gave me something to drink,
I was a stranger and you invited me in,
I needed clothes and you clothed me,
I was in prison and you came to visit me.

—Matthew 25:35–36 NIV

God took care of me when I was still far off.

The Bible Rebellion

The Bible is one of the few treasured possessions that the women carry from camp to camp. My mother's Dutch bible is big and black. My Dutch grandmother gave it to her before she embarked on a new future with a new husband in the faraway tropical Dutch East Indies.

The small verse written by my grandmother on the front page may almost have been prophetic.

> As humans we often suffer most
> Through the suffering of all that we are afraid of,
> But mostly those things never happen;
> Too much of our suffering is of our own making,
> More than God will ever give us to carry.

All our belongings have to be carried in the flimsy cardboard suitcases by the women themselves. Their bibles are big and heavy but the women will take them from camp to camp.

Without any other distractions available, the people in the camps live close to God. His words uphold them, give them a future, make them feel loved amidst the unloveliness of war, and give them hope and fellowship in these dark days.

The Nippon knows this. Services are forbidden, and so are prayers. But there are plenty of women who defy these rules, and their bibles are part of their strength of character.

A Nippon will find any excuse to punish the women, and today is no exception. Often the so-called crime is so small and insignificant as to be laughable. There is, of course, nothing very laughable about it if through punishment food is withheld from our already starvation ration of one cup of water-lily soup with rice.

Today every bible in the camp is to be confiscated. A Japanese *tjap*—or stamp—together with our personal camp number will be entered in our big black Dutch bible before it is handed over to the commander. We have to display our camp number on all our possessions as well as on ourselves. Each member of our little family wears a narrow linen band on his or her wrist with the number II 14688 upon it.

But today the punishment is the confiscating of our bibles. Thousands of Bibles are dumped in a *goedang*, a store room. So angry and indignant are the women that for many hours they talk and discuss little else. Finally they decide to send a delegation to see Sonei, the camp commander. Each house has chosen its own leader. The small group of leader representatives arrives at the commander's office, where of course they obey all the rules expected from them. They bow deeply and remain in that position until told to speak.

They speak courteously but determinedly and ask for the bibles to be returned. Few know about the Geneva Convention, but all know that, even here in this hell hole, this so-called punishment is unacceptable. They also know that if the women persist in their request for the return of the bibles, the Nippon may well decide on further, much worse punishment, and the entire camp may be forced to have 'hunger days'. Hunger days mean no food at all for up to three days in a row. All inmates save tiny portions of their already meagre rations for those frequently occurring hunger days. Rarely can they save for more than one day.

There may also be beatings for punishment, and any person will do if volunteers are not forthcoming. Despite these possibilities, the women courageously continue their courteous but determined argument.

The Japanese culture expects women to be submissive and servile, and Sonei is at loss as to how to deal with these determined Dutch women. Eventually, and quite unexpectedly, Sonei relents, and to the joy of all, the bibles are returned. Once again, the inexplicable character of the Jap is displayed.

It is only as I have got older that I have come to see this as another example of God's grace shining, through the courage and conviction of the women, to even those men riddled with evil.

I now own that bible, and when I see our camp number, II 14688, together with the Japanese stamp and my grandmother's wise words, I realize that God will always deal with His people in grace. He was there protecting me, loving me, and caring for me long before I knew about Him and when I was still a long way off.

The Breaking of the Shell

Anoint the wounds of my spirit with the balm of forgiveness,
Pour the oil of your calm on the waters of my heart,
Take the squeal of frustration from the wheels of my passion
That the power of your tenderness may smooth the way I love
That the tedium of giving in the risk of surrender
And the reaching out naked to a world that must wound,
May be kindled fresh daily to a blaze of compassion, may fall gladly
to burst in the ground and the harvest abound

—Dom Ralph Wright

Royalty In A Concentration Camp

We own few possessions, but we carry photographs of our fathers with us from camp to camp. I only know a father without legs, as the picture of my handsome, dark-skinned father only shows his head and shoulders.

At the end of the war, we children see our pappies for the first time in three and a half years. I recall seeing these men in khaki walking into the camp. Nicolette and I go to find our mammie, shouting at the top of our voices, 'Mammie, Mammie, the daddies have come, the daddies with legs!' Pappies as far as we know them are not related to real people; they are just photographs.

So it is also with royalty. The Dutch women are fiercely royalist, and many photographs of our beloved Queen, Wilhelmina, are secretly tucked behind the pictures of our fathers.

The Japs are insatiably curious about relationships and are often questioning the women about the photographs. So they lie blatantly, pronouncing the picture of the queen or her daughter, Juliana, to be their mother, or sister, or aunty. Sometimes, to the hilarity of those watching, Princess Juliana will become 'my husband's second wife'—quite acceptable in an Islamic country! Prince Bernhard becomes a brother or uncle. What do the Japs know?

The same goes with the Dutch tricolour flag. The three colours are picked apart and kept in separate places. The Japs are always questioning everything: 'So, what are these pieces of cloth?'

'Oh, just to make into new clothes.' But in reality the colours of our flag are never used for anything other than to keep up the women's courage, patriotic expression, and hope.

The Japs do not speak our language, and to trick them the women have devised a way of saying the Dutch National anthem in a conversational tone: 'Wilhelmus van Nassaue, mijn schild en de betrouwe, de tyrannie verdrijven,' and so on.

The V for Victory is also used in disguise. Here is a ditty made up for the sole reason of defiantly using the V.

Val om!	Fall over!
Val dood!	Fall down dead!
Val krom!	Fall down crookedly!
Val neer!	Fall down!
Verrek!	Blast you!
Verroest!	Blow you!
Verrot!	Rot you!
Verteer!	Disintegrate!

This ditty can be sung with gusto, and no Nippon will ever suspect it is directed at them!

All these secret communications keep the women going, their sense of humour intact, and their sense of self-worth, in view of so much humiliation, above par. But even more, it keeps a sense of unity in the face of so much appalling adversity. All the situations that are completely inhumane and yet unchangeable are turned into mockery.

The Nippon staff are all given nicknames. Most of them are ludicrous and often have to do with the way they behave. There is Mr Purple Head; he always goes puce from all the screaming he does. Mr Peeping Tom, he likes to come into our communal bathroom, shouting unreasonable commands, just when the women are stripped down for a wash. Mr Giant is so diminutive that most of the Dutch women tower over him.

In Tjideng the Nippon suddenly demands that any bicycles still remaining in the camp are going to be confiscated. But within twenty-four hours every child is set to destroy a bicycle. Spokes are removed and used for knitting needles. All parts are salvaged, and those bits that cannot be reused are drenched in water. Twenty-four hours later the Nippon have lots of rusty components but no bicycles!

There is a steeliness present in many of the Dutch women, a will to survive. Optimism is quite out of proportion to the pitiful existence and isolation within the walls of the countless camps.

The Japanese have set up three hundred concentration camps around the archipelago of the colony. Most contain women and children, as many of the men have been sent to build the railway through the jungle of Burma. Many of the European women have only experienced luxurious pre-war existences.

They have all lived with four or five (or more) live-in staff to deal with every whim these colonial women could dream up. And yet they do not give up now. There is no room for sentimentality, self-pity, or selfishness. Instead, life is lived facing reality, with a sense of pride and selflessness that goes far beyond the confines of family or friends.

There is a remarkable discovery of ingenuity in every women and child, which helps us to survive and use every source available. Everything is recycled many times over.

Birthdays are celebrated in typical Dutch fashion. Everyone brings a gift, no matter how minute or how useless. But in any case, it is an excuse to celebrate and break the monotony of camp life. Boredom and monotony are the greatest curse of life here.

Education is forbidden, but there are no resources for education anyway.

The medical staff has learned to experiment with plants, bark, and juices. Their courage to defend their patients against the Nippon inhumanity has become legendary. Some of the medical staff defy the orders from camp commanders to bring out the sick into the tropical heat of the sun for the three-hour sessions of silent bowing in front of the cruel hierarchy of the camp. Many a time the request for quinine or other simple medication has been rewarded with a beating, and yet doctors or nurses return time and again to plead for their patients. The general attitude of the Nippon is that a patient will eat but not work, so the sooner they are dead the better.

The women, in proper Dutch fashion, take meticulous care of their few belongings, their clothing, and their bodies. Few of the children wear shoes, and the communal loos are no more than holes in the ground with a few planks across. Great care has to be taken, especially with small children, not to fall into the cesspits, which are crawling with maggots. As a modern child is taught to wash hands after visiting the loo, we are taught to wash our feet to remove the crawling maggots.

My Mammie carries our mats outside each morning to shake them out and leave them in the sun to sterilize them and minimize lice, bedbugs, or other creatures that may inhabit.

It is this constant busyness, this meticulous routine in small ways, that keeps the women reasonably happy and gives them a sense of usefulness that sets them apart from the male camp dwellers. Together with their sense of protectiveness towards their children, the women have reason to keep alive, keep going, and keep life in perspective.

The ordinariness of small household tasks also keeps their sense of humour intact. There is lots of fun and humour. Their sense of the ridiculous towards their captors is most likely the most important single factor that binds them together.

No one ever doubts that ultimately good will overcome evil. We will be the victors. Dutch women are like grass. No matter how you trample it, it will recover and grow again.

As for us children, we trust and accept.

Camp Snails

Nicolette and I do everything together. She holds my hand as we go round the camp or perform the tasks that Mammie has given us. There is little to do for the children of the camps, but we all have small responsibilities. Nicolette and I have been given a tin bucket to collect snails. Snail-hunting is an occupation all camp children are familiar with, and we hunt them with a passion. Snails are the only meat we know, and there is fierce competition between the occupants of each overcrowded house to collect as many as possible. Nicolette and I look under stones, in cracks on walls, and by the drain that runs away from the *mandi*, the communal washing place.

Other than human beings, the camp is almost entirely devoid of living things. Any creature that moves will be hunted down until caught and added to the cooking pots. There is the story of the women watching a heron slowly fly over the camp, carrying a large fish in its beak. With great presence of mind, the woman quickly and loudly clapped her hands, at which the heron dropped its prey, right by the woman's feet.

After years of being hunted down by small children, there are few creatures left. Snakes, rats, mice, geckos, dogs, or cats—all have gone. However there seems a never-ending supply of snails, and we little ones are good at sniffing them out!

The sucking sound of a snail being pulled off its place of abode is unlike anything else in the world and most pleasing to my ears. As the little creatures slowly wind their way back onto the side of the bucket, I gently pull them away from the metal, and the little house hits the floor once again. I love watching them patiently track back up the side, and sometimes I will let them have a race. I will put two or three side by side on the bucket floor, and here they go ...

There is always this terrible conflict of watching the gentle creatures, their shiny feelers communicating a trust in my presence. At the same time, there is the ever-present gnawing pain of hunger in the pit of my stomach. There is little room for sentimentality in our lives.

Nevertheless, there is the awful knowledge of deceit just round the corner. I know that my little friends are going to die, and I know I am going to watch in fascination when they do so.

Nicolette is getting quite cross and impatient with me. 'Ajo, Han'—hurry up—she says, and we carry the bucket between us to the kitchen ladies. We watch as they drop the shiny houses into the boiling water in the oil drum we use for cooking. I hear the sizzling air bubbles escaping from each little house before it becomes still. Sometimes Mammie rewards us with a small piece of coloured glass or a pretty stone.

Many years later, snails are the bane of my life as I watch them eat my young seedlings and my lush vegetables in the kitchen garden. Even the soft fruit in the fruit cage are overrun with the silvery tracks left by a multitude of snails. But I will never be able to squash them. I can only pick them off and throw them into the adjoining field, hoping they will stay there. I will always love the small multi-coloured stripy cases left by them or, indeed, even the giant land snails found on the African plains. Finding them always gives me a thrill.

Nicolette and I have a treasured collection of stones. We play at tea parties or shops of which we really have no concept, but with the older girls' help, we make believe and pretend at cups and saucers fashioned from grasses and leaves, with sticks for spoons.

We have never eaten cake or biscuits or seen pretty china. We each have a tin mug and plate and spoon, and most of our food is eaten by squashing the rice into little balls before popping these into our mouths. Just as the locals do, we eat with our fingers. Every tiny crumb or grain is savoured to make it last longer, and our palates are quite unsophisticated. Eating takes a long time, despite the tiny rations.

We are always hungry, and there is a real pain in our stomachs. It's quite different from being hungry on a well-supplied diet. My legs are often wobbly, and I have to sit down for a long time while I wait for the shakiness to go.

Mammie has recorded in my baby book that on 26 May 1943 we received a rare gift of an American Red Cross parcel; this day will be etched into my mind forever. I have never before eaten meat or cheese, and I am so excited that I cannot stop talking. 'I am eating cheese and meat! I am eating cheese and meat!' I am banging my spoon onto the tin plate while delighting in watching my siblings sample this rare delight. The meat comes from a tin and is called corned beef. The tin has a little metal loop on the side, which Mammie pulls to open it. It has a picture of a brown cow with long horns. I have never seen a cow, but the corned beef is the best thing I have ever tasted.

The Bread Cart

During the last year of the war food is the most talked-about subject in the camp. It occupies our thinking all day long. The women spend many hours discussing recipes with each other. Most of the women in the camp have only ever had a kokkie (cook) in their kitchens and simply instructed kokkie on what to buy at the market and what to cook for that day's lunch. But in the camp they have all learned what to cook and how to cook by simply talking about it. The women call it 'ghost cooking'. They salivate at the very thought of all the things they will eat when the war is over, the dishes they will concoct.

When I questioned my mother many years later about these ghost meals they would produce, she told me how their recipes became more and more elaborate and amazing. Surely they would be able to produce complete banquets after the war!

There are no fat people in the camp after almost three years on a starvation diet. As for the children, our palates are utterly unsophisticated. We have no idea what the women are talking about, as we have never tasted any of the foods they are discussing and remembering in such animated ways. We have lived our entire lives on tiny portions of tasteless rice soups and the very occasional slice of bread. We chew everything over slowly to make the food last as long as possible.

I have vivid memories of my very first tastes of the most simple foods after the war. I can recall in detail where and when I was eating my first slice of cheese, my first apple, and my first drink of fresh milk. Each occasion was a momentous time of my life.

One morning, at the time of a full moon, Camp Commander Sonei has gone into one of his mad modes again. He has commanded a group of women to start digging a pit so large and so deep that many of them are quite sure they have come to the end and are being asked to dig their own grave. The ground is rock hard, and the women are weak from malnutrition. They take it in turn to dig and sweat profusely in the burning tropical sun. It takes many hours to dig the huge pit to the satisfaction of Sonei, and the women wonder what is going to happen next. They are told to stand on the parade ground and wait.

Many hours pass, and then they are ordered to return to the giant pit. Slowly but surely the gates into the camp are opened, and a very large cart pulled by two bullocks is drawn into the camp. The cart is piled high with hundreds of loaves of fragrant, freshly baked bread.

The women are astounded, and their spirits are lifted. Sonei has done some appalling things to the occupants of the Tjideng camp, and they are wondering whether his humanity has finally overcome his evil. They smile at the very thought of this change of heart. The women start to talk excitedly, but the soldiers scream their displeasure and use their whips on those nearest to them to silence them.

When the bullocks arrive at the huge pit, Sonei shouts instructions at the soldiers. To the shocked horror, fury, and utter disbelief of the exhausted, hungry women, the soldiers begin to pull the loaves off the cart and start tipping them into the pit. The soldiers jump into the pit on top of the loaves and begin to stamp on them, smashing them into pulp. One by one, each loaf is dispatched into the pit and macerated by the boots of the soldiers.

The hungry women and children watch in silence as this act of sheer cruelty and vandalism continues. It is beyond comprehension that one human being can torture another human being to this degree. When the cart is emptied, the women are ordered to cover the loaves and fill the pit with the soil they dug out.

This day will go down in the minds of the women as one of the lowest points of the war. There are almost no words for this inhumane degradation of even the most optimistic and sanguine of those incarcerated in Tjideng.

The Final Year

As a small girl, my hand is filled with very little. On Java, the starry nights are full of wonder, and it is a game between us that whoever sees the first twinkling star in the evening sky may ask for a wish. It is one of those small pleasures in my life that I look forward to.

In the camps we have learned to share whatever we have. Even food is meticulously shared, despite the constant feeling of hunger that never leaves us. No one would dream of being greedy and taking one grain of rice more than a neighbour.

This is the final year that Tjideng is being tortured by Camp Commandant Sonei. His moon madness manifests itself in a regime of terror. The butcher of Tjideng takes sadistic pleasure in torturing the inmates. Wearing only his see-through kimono, he screams and orders his soldiers, 'Lekas, lekas!—quick, quick!' His face contorted with madness, his wildly gesticulating arms brandish his long whip that sweeps across the nearest person, soldier or inmate, leaving him or her severely bruised and battered.

More and more frequently his order is for all to get out of bed for a midnight parade. The soldiers walk into bedrooms and sleeping places, yelling commands at the jam-packed rooms, threatening punishments and shouting obscenities if orders are not obeyed at once.

Terrified and tired, children scream while sleepy mothers hastily dress their little ones to steer them out into the dark night, where they shuffle into neat rows while the Nippon continue to shriek their abuse.

The cool of the tropical night and the starry night has a calming effect on me, and soon the twinkling stars and the mighty Milky Way have my attention. I start searching for a falling star that will allow me to say a wish.

Sonei's obsession with hunger days, too, come more frequently now. Three days without food, while Sonei openly buries three days of rations for ten thousand people into large pits dug by the women themselves, is obscene.

There is a longing for peace. Mammie writes in my baby book: 'How much longer will this war last? Please, God, let peace come soon.'

Women and children have become a mass of humanity. We are only numbers, with no names, no individuality. The women are so tired. Too many have already died. In order to survive, both large and small, old and young have learned to obey. To do otherwise is suicide. We respond collectively, and we care for each other collectively. We count small mercies, we encourage each other, we pray, and we hope. When nothing of our human veneer is left and all the chips are down, God's love is all that remains to hold onto.

The death toll this last year of the war is rising, especially among the children of the camps. We know now that elimination is the Nippons' target. Their racial hatred against their European fellow men is their motivation.

The war in Europe has come to an end in May 1945 —but for us the pacific war rages on. Does the world not know what atrocities are being committed in these far ends of the world? Although this is a world war, the islands are under no scrutiny from press or camera crews. It will be many years before the truth of another genocide, far removed from the death camps in Europe, will receive some recognition.

There are few Jews among us, and no one has coined the words *ethnic cleansing* yet. But this is what our elimination has become. Still, among the ugliness of war and hatred, God's grace is working in people's lives.

In the final Easter week in Tjideng, permission is given for a silent service; no singing or praying out loud will be allowed. In a world where noise due to overcrowding; crying, hungry children; and screaming soldiers is commonplace, silence has become a very rare commodity. Silence is seen as a precious gift of God.

When we are in the depths of despair, we learn to cry out to God. There are some deep truths about ourselves that only sorrow can teach us. It is only through sorrow that we can reach some unfathomable depths of our own beings, through becoming open to God. God's grace is here, in the midst of the chaos, the hunger, the overcrowding, the deaths, and the humiliations. And God uses his grace, through the faith of others, in the most unexpected places and touching the most unlikely people.

All week the women of Tjideng have taken their buckets and mops and dusters and have, in proper Dutch fashion, cleaned the church in readiness for the Easter service. There is no thought of denominational division, and Roman, Dutch Reformed, Buddhist, Hindu, Anglican, and Baptist have gathered for a service. The Roman Catholic nuns in the hospital have baked tiny yeastless loaves, and from somewhere a bottle of rice wine has been found and watered down to make it go round.

The doors of the church have been left wide open, and halfway through the silent service, a Japanese officer walks up the steps, his sword trailing behind him and clattering on the marble tiles. He sits in the back of the church, folding his arms and burying his face. He cries—he sits and cries for fifteen minutes before leaving the church and returning to his duties. He is unaware of the stirring of the women's hearts or the noise his sword makes accompanying his exit. He is a human being full of sadness in the presence of God.

C. S. Lewis said that pain is God's megaphone to arouse a deaf world. God's grace does move in mysterious ways.

Prang Soedah Abis, 15 August 1945

'The war is over.'

There are aeroplanes in the sky—great big, droning planes. Some are American, some are English, and the occasional one is Dutch. The planes fly towards the north-west, and the rumour goes that this means *prang soedah abis*—the war is over!

There is a feeling of excitement in the camp, but contrary to feelings, nothing has so far changed for the better—rather the opposite. Food rations are smaller every day. Nippon expects the women to work harder, and the whip is used constantly and with vehemence. The Japs are continuously hitting out, and there is a great deal of nervous energy that manifests itself in more and more violence. Sonei, knowing his days are numbered, has become like the devil incarnate.

The women on the other hand, knowing something is up have become almost reckless in their dealings with the outside world.

Gedekking, the bartering for food through the barb-wire-and-bamboo fencing, is rife, and Sonei seizes his final chance. Four hundred women (mostly volunteers) are paraded in front of the whole silent camp while one after another has her hair hacked off with blunt scissors.

When the English soldiers finally liberate us, they quickly realize that Sunny boy (Sonei's nickname) will be lynched by the surviving women in no time, so within hours he is taken away to be tried for his war crimes, before the women have a chance to cut him to pieces.

Finally there is a real sense of liberation, as all adults and children alike rip apart the matting fence that has surrounded the camp for so long. There is a future out there, and those of us who have survived the three and a half years of horror can see beyond the confines of camp life.

I am only a small girl, but it takes no time at all to sense a freedom, a new atmosphere, and I carry away the strips of bamboo in great triumph.

Jesus said, 'Blessed are the poor,' and whatever the years of deprivation have done to me, many years later I have realized that the blessing that has come out of all the horror is just that—a blessing. Deprive people of their human rights, humiliate, torture, and oppress them, but this process of depravation will produce men, women, and children of extraordinary spirit and strength.

Many more years of humiliation await me during my lifetime. Those early years of my life were merely a preparation for me, to enable me to cope with life's sorrows.

It is through the storms that rage through our lifetimes that we learn to catch glimpses of the calm within ourselves. The essence of our real selves waits to be discovered, through the storms of life.

The Singapore War Tribunals

Soon after the Pacific war finished, our Tjideng Camp Commander Sonei, the butcher of Tjideng was taken to Singapore where he was to face the war tribunals.

Sonei was the son of a Japanese father and a German mother.

In September 1945, Captain Kenichi Sonei was convicted of war crimes and sentenced to death.

The sentence was carried out by a ten man Dutch Army squad in December 1945

Learning To See New Emotions

My Aunty Maud (not a real aunty, but in the camp every woman is an aunty), who is English, has taught me how to say, 'How do you do, Daddy.' It is the first English I learn, and I repeat it over and over again. Mammie tells me to be quiet, as she is fed up with it. But after a short time I forget the request and start all over again with 'How do you do, Daddy.'

Then one day the war is 'soedah abis'. A bomb has been dropped on Japan, but details are sketchy...

The Allied soldiers have taken charge and have put the Japanese soldiers to work the Nippon have suddenly become courteous and polite to the inmates of the camp. Orange, red, white, and blue have come out of hiding, and no one threatens punishment for displaying our national colours. It is 23 August, and the first Dutch doctors are entering the camps.

A young doctor sits on our mats, and although he is a grown man, we watch in amazement when emotion overcomes him and big tears fill his eyes and roll down his red, fresh, young face.

He sits and just looks at us, shaking his head repeatedly, letting his eyes take in the horror of what he is seeing, but we are quite unaware of the pitiful sight we are to this healthy person.

A woman and her three small children, all so thin, we are no more than bags of bones. We have almost no hair, there are tropical ulcers on our bodies and under our hair, and our eyes are huge in our hollow, yellow faces. My mother always maintained that at that stage she did not think we had much more than a few weeks left to live.

Our lethargy is so unnatural in young children that the man just sits and shakes his head. He carries a bag that contains medicines and tells us he will give us all vitamin injections. This is a new word and a new concept—a man who has come to be friendly.

Whatever this vitamin injection is, we can tell it is good. I watch in fascination when he brings out the metal syringe and sticks the big needle into a small, dumpy bottle with a rubber seal, to pull up the liquid. It is all a mystery to me. I do not think of the pain, just the kindness, the tears, and the compassion. It is an emotion so new, so unheard of among the toughness, cheerfulness, and camaraderie of the women. It's so unknown among the only other men we have known in our young lives, the Nippon, that it is something I shall never forget.

The doctor says he will come back again in a week's time and bring more vitamin injections. It does not matter to us that the needle hurts, because this young doctor is kind and calls us by our names, and brings us pieces of chocolate in silvery bits of paper that are almost as valuable as the chocolate itself.

In the camps we owned nothing, growing up without toys or books, pens or paper. We learned to play in our imaginations. We also lived in very close communities and learned to be aware of people's feelings, suppressed irritations, anger, cruelty, unfairness, love, generosity, fun, and joy. We learned first-hand about sickness and death on a daily basis. We learned about emotions and how to avoid them. I suppose in many ways we learned to be sensitive and show empathy and to be careful so as not to rock the boat.

Sensitivity has always been part of the way I relate to people. It has also plagued me, as so often my oversensitivity played a very negative part in my marriage. Sensitivity is a gift of God, but it is also a two-edged sword. It cuts deeply both ways. It empowers us to respond to the hurts and needs and sorrows of others, but it also makes us feel more deeply the hurts that others inflict upon us. We need to look to God to help us find the balance.

What Happened To The Chocolate

The first week after the English and Australian soldiers enter the camp, we are given a Red Cross parcel. There is a tin of corned beef, and I am so excited because Mammie tells us that this is *meat!* and it is very good for us. I have only once before eaten meat, apart from the snails we collect, and that was when we received the American Red Cross parcel. I am banging my spoon on the tin plate and learning to enjoy new food and tastes. Oh, what a happy atmosphere!

There is also chocolate in the parcel, but we children will never see any of it! Mammie has spotted it and before we do, she hides it. Many years later she recalls the shame of it! She rightly guessed that we would not know about the delights of chocolate and so we would not feel deprived if she ate it all by herself!

That night, while we are asleep, she eats a tiny piece of it. Savouring the delicious taste and with every intention to make it last for a number of days, she settles down to sleep. Alas, the first piece tastes so good that she cannot sleep for thinking about the pieces left. So she consumes a second piece, and another, and another—till it's all gone! However, our stomachs have shrunk from years of having been on a starvation diet. A large bar of chocolate will have the most disastrous effect. Mammie always claimed that despite her terrible guilt feelings and despite the appalling stomach cramps and the diarrhoea, it was all worth it!

Our beloved tricolour can be displayed again, and the flag can be seen throughout the camp, hanging from washing lines and draped over people's shoulders. But the truth is that we cannot leave the camps. Ethnic cleansing is on its way, and our white faces are incitement to murder.

The Japanese have mixed up all our personal information, and those who have survived the camps will have to wait, often for weeks or months, before being reunited with their loved ones. Many, of course, have died, and many children have been left parentless. Our grandparents have died too, and it will be another fifty years or so before I find their grave in Salatiga, mid Java.

Pappies Home Coming January 1946

RAPWI (Relief of Allied Prisoners of War and Internees), together with the Red Cross, wade through unending information in an attempt to reunite families. The Japs have for years moved us relentlessly among the three hundred or so concentration camps they have set up on the many islands. During the weeks and months following our freedom, it is unsafe for Europeans to be seen outside the camps.

The Japanese propaganda machine has turned the indigenous population against the colonial regime, and it is not safe for any *belanda* (white-faced European) to be out and about. So we remain in the hated camps. Although we are being fed and protected by the Allied soldiers, we still sleep in cramped conditions and are confined within prison walls.

There is huge resentment among the women, who have been dreaming of not just freedom but husbands, pretty new dresses, make-up, privacy, homeland, little luxuries, space, and many such things. We remain in Tjideng, and five months later have not yet met up with our father.

In January 1946, we are finally reunited with our father. My pappie finds us still in the chaos and hideous conditions in Tjideng. This is the first time he has seen his son. He received a Red Cross card telling him of the birth of his son while he was working on the Burma–Thai railway, a whole year after Frank was born.

I remember looking at this stranger and just smiling and smiling and smiling. In his KNIL (Royal Netherlands East Indies Army) khaki uniform he looks so handsome. He has very dark and hairy arms and legs and is very tall. The Nippon have almost no body hair and are quite short, so this man is definitely different.

It is a wonder for me to see our father as a real person and not just a photograph. From his breast pocket he produces for me the very first present I have ever received. It is a small khaki army mirror. The mirror is a shiny metal surface. It is really mine—and I can look at myself for the very first time. "Don't look too long in the mirror, Hanneke, or your hair will turn green!" I polish it on a corner of my shorts, and it will remain a treasured gift for many years to come. There is a wonderful feeling of wholeness among our family.

But the *permoedas*—(often very young) boys indoctrinated by the Japanese to hate all former colonials—go on the rampage during this time. It is not safe for any of us. There is a Communist uprising brewing.

Balikpapan On The Island Of Borneo, March 1946

We are on the move again. We have packed our meagre belongings and are waiting for transport. We have moved so often that we consider another move as a normal part of our nomadic life. However, this time it is going to be different. We shall have our pappie with us. He does not live with us, as he is still a serving soldier with the Royal Dutch East Indies Army, so after each visit he goes back to his barracks. But today we are all going to move together.

Nicolette, Frank, and I are sitting in the shade of the huge mango tree, waiting patiently for things to happen. We look like different children now. After just a few months of eating proper food, we have filled out, our sores have gone, our hair has grown glossy, and our energy levels are approaching normal. The kind doctor has come back many times to give us weekly vitamin injections and something of a wonder medicine for the festering sores. It is called penicillin.

I am wearing a real dress, the very first dress I have ever possessed. We little ones have only ever worn shorts, made from old faded dresses discarded by grown-ups. The dress is royal-blue cotton, with wide straps over my shoulders and a band of red and white flowers across the top.

I am also wearing shoes, provided by the Red Cross ladies. They are made of leather and have straps with a buckle. They are called sandals, and I do not find them very comfortable after having walked on bare feet all my life. But Mammie insists we wear them, as she is concerned we pick up small skin-burrowing worms that eat away the soles of our feet. All the locals suffer from them. It does not seem to do them any harm, but suddenly our European ancestry has become important again, and Europeans have to wear shoes!

We sit and wait and do not mind the waiting. In the camps we have learned to be patient, and so we sit quietly without moving or having anything to occupy us. We have said our goodbyes and now simply sit and watch those of our friends who will be moving with us bring out their few belongings. We hug those we leave behind.

At long last a big khaki lorry arrives. Our pappie is already sitting on the long bench in the back, and he jumps out to help us on board. He collects the single battered cardboard suitcase that holds our whole family's belongings and then passes each of us to the waiting arms of another soldier. The lorry is full of other people and soldiers carrying guns. This will be a dangerous journey, and we need the protection of the soldiers.

A big canvas tent hides us from being seen. The children sit on the floor, while the adults sit on the metal benches. This will be my first journey in an automobile, and whatever the danger, it is very exciting. We go very fast, and I can feel the hot wind rushing through the gaps in the canvas.

At last we arrive, and before us stretches a vast tarmac apron with aeroplanes everywhere. They are huge and khaki coloured, and I can see some steps leading to the door of the aeroplane we are going to fly in. It is like nothing I have ever seen before. I have been told it will fly like a bird in the sky and we will sit in its tummy. But it is so big! How will it get off the ground, and how will it flap its wings? There is no time for questions; we are hastily handed down from the truck, while a ring of soldiers stand in a large semicircle facing outwards, with their guns at the ready, protecting us. But all our lives we have been surrounded by soldiers, and so we are not alarmed at all. When everyone has descended from the truck, we all move quickly to the waiting plane. The steps up to the door are made of shiny metal, with round holes so that I can look through, down to the tarmac below." Hurry, hurry, Hanneke! It is too dangerous to stop and look around you."

The inside of the plane is a huge place. There are no seats, just benches along one side. There are round windows and lots of khaki webbing lying about in great heaps everywhere. The plane is a bomber. It has been used all through the war, but now it is used for transporting families to different islands where the permoedas are not so active.

When the door is closed, the noise of the engines is so overwhelming that it terrifies me. We have lived for many years without hearing any mechanical noises, and this aeroplane makes a noise quite unlike anything I have ever heard. Mammie crinkles up her eyes and gives me a reassuring nod. The kind soldiers keep smiling and nodding their heads as if to say, 'It is all right. We are not afraid, nor should you be.' It is called trust, and I suppose children trust adults, however strange the surroundings.

But that's not all. We have each been given a sweet! 'For your ears'—whatever that may mean! The sweet is red and very hard and sharp-tasting, and if I suck it carefully, it lasts for a very long time. I soon settle into a peaceful dream world as the droning sound of the aeroplane quietens me. In any case, the noise is so loud that we cannot hear each other when we speak.

We finally arrive at our destination, and the huge plane goes bump, bump, bump over the tarmac until it comes to a stop. Then the big door is opened, and the hot air hits us when we emerge. On the edge of the tarmac the jungle starts, and I can see a fringe of tall coconut trees gently waving in the wind. We wave goodbye to the kind soldiers, and a new group leads us to another army truck.

This is Balikpapan, on the island of Borneo. This is a safe place, and the truck we board has no canvas so that we can see what is around us. Our home is going to be an enormous dark-green tent. It has two rooms and a big flysheet to provide plenty of shade. A mosquito net serves as a door. Mammie has her own room, and we three children share a room. Pappie has to go back to barracks; he is only a visitor for the time being. There are no mattresses or mats to sleep on, but we are each given our own bed. They are camp beds, but nevertheless, we each have a bed to ourselves. It is the first time we have slept on beds, so we are very excited.

We are classified as refugees now. The refugee tent camp is right on a golden stretch of beach, and we can see lots of other tents and a wire fence. Unlike at the camps on Java, this fence is not there to keep us in; it is there to keep intruders out. Soldiers walk the perimeter. There are coconut trees all along the edge of the beach, which produce plenty of shade. Not only do we have beds, but there is also a small square table and two rattan chairs. The place is like a palace to us, and we soon kick off our shoes and run to the beach.

The beach is a paradise too. There are treasures free for the taking. Shells are everywhere: cowries, with smooth, dark-brown, shiny, spotted surfaces, and some other bright-pink ones. Others are rough on the outside and polished on the inside. There are big ones and tiny ones, round ones, and ones with delicate projecting arms. Each and every one is an object of beauty and wonder.

It is the beginning of my love affair with shells, and I collect everything I see. Very soon there is a wonderful collection of shells large and small lying all round our tent, which we arrange and rearrange in pleasing patterns on the white beach sands.

We may swim and paddle but only under supervision of servants. There are poisonous sea snakes in these warm tropical seas. In reality, the snakes are gentle creatures who do not attack human beings. Besides, their mouths are so small they could hardly bite sufficiently to deliver enough poison.

Many years later, I will return to these waters, to swim and snorkel and discover the delights, abundance, and beauty of the shallow coral reefs and the 'water gardens', as the locals call this place.

But this is the tropics, and Mammie calls us back. We are not allowed out in the sun in the middle of the day. A dusting of fine white talcum powder is sprinkled onto arms and shoulders to protect our skin from the sun.

This is a new rule. We have been accustomed to standing in the midday sun for many hours without any protection during the Jap occupation. How quickly civilization is returning to our lives.

Life In A Refugee Camp

We have been in the tented camp for a few months now. Life has settled into a kind of routine, and we have quickly slipped into old habits. We have a *djongos*. He is a local man who has become our servant. He is 'local' in that he goes home each night to his own kampong or village. The servants we had before the war all lived in. They lived on the *blakan*, or servant's quarters, at the back of the house.

It seems odd that we should have a servant at all when we live in a tent in a refugee camp, but Pappie says that now war is over we should try and go back to some life of normality. To Europeans, that includes servants.

Our servant's name is Budi, but we all call him Djongos. Djongos smokes *kretek* cigarettes. They are spicy homemade ones. We watch in fascination as Djongos rolls a tiny bit of shredded tobacco together with ground cloves in *klabot* (the young leaves of the *djagoen* or sweet corn). The cigarette is rolled into a conical shape and held together with a tiny snippet of coloured cotton. All the locals smoke kretek cigarettes, and the spicy smell pervades the air with a lovely aroma. The smell is part of my childhood, and there is nothing like it anywhere else in the world.

We are always questioning Budi: Why does he smoke? What is it like? Can we have a little puff, or at least have a go at rolling one? But Djongos good-naturedly grins, revealing his filthy yellow teeth, and patiently tells us again and again that cigarettes are *not* for children. When he has finished smoking, he flicks away the tiny pointed end of the cigarette.

Frank is only 4 years old, but he is mischievous and adventurous. Unbeknown to Nicolette and me, he has watched Djongos every time he has rolled and smoked and finally flicked away the remains into the sand. Frank has been collecting the fag ends, and now he keeps them in a secret place.

Our collection of shells lives at the bottom of a tall coconut tree not far from our tent. Stuffed inside a long, spiky shell are the remains of Budi's fag ends. What a perfect hiding place! No one would look twice at the pile of shells. We talk and plot and plan. We have to wait for the pile to be large enough to make our own cigarette, and then we have to find some matches.

I have begged Djongos for some cotton, ostensibly to tie together a bunch of small flowers. The piece of cotton will serve to tie up our home-made cigarette when we have got all the ingredients. We still live in a world of shortages, and it will soon be discovered if matches go missing. But Nicolette has found some, and they, too, are hidden in our secret place. Nicolette is the oldest, and it is she who finally rolls our cigarette and lights it.

Our father smokes also. His cigarettes are white; they come from a round tin with gold lettering on it and a yellow animal called a camel pictured on the side. So we have watched and know that we have to inhale the smoke and blow it out again. We hide behind the tent and take it in turn having a puff, while being advised by the others.

However, our territory is not very big and before we know it, Mammie has come to see what is going on. She has a quick temper and instantly reads us the riot act. She will teach us a lesson!

As soon as Pappie returns home, they confer, and before we know it, we are sitting in a row on one of the canvas camp beds. 'Here, sit here, and we will teach you to smoke.'

We are each presented with a cigarette from the round tin. 'You will sit and stay and smoke till the cigarette is gone and you are as sick as a dog.'

Very aware of our misdemeanour, we sit and puff away. Both Nicolette and I are soon feeling sick and looking green, but there is no let-up. This is going to be a lesson that we shall not forget.

Little Frank, however, is enjoying the smoke and is quite unperturbed by it. Soon our parents realize that this lesson is not an unqualified success.

They are still laughing at themselves till late into the night at this most unconventional, misfired lesson in life.

Makassar On The Island Of Celebes

We have moved again, and now we live in a real house. It has a sitting room, a *mandi* (bathroom), a dining room, three bedrooms, and a big veranda.

Makassar is an old harbour town. The wharf is wide and goes on and on. There are many beautiful wooden sailing ships, all painted white. They carry cargo between the thousands of islands that make up the archipelago. This is a very hot and humid place, with temperatures seldom below thirty-five Celsius. There is always something to be seen, and we often walk along the quayside to admire the prows of the white ships lined up and piled high with cargo.

Makassar has for many centuries been the centre of shipbuilding, and besides the noise of hammering, sawing of timber planks, and shouting of people, there is lots to see: huge piles of coconut, jute sacks full of smelly dried fish, and sacks full of garlic or kapok.

We especially enjoy watching the sailmakers at work. The giant sails, many of which are brown, are laid out on the quay, and as many as twenty sailmakers work on one sail. They work in the burning sun, hats pulled over their ears, talking and laughing incessantly. '*Pagi, toean,*' they call in unison when they see our father in his smart white trousers and long-sleeved shirt.

We now not only have a djongos but also a maid, called *Baboe*. All the maids are always called Baboe. Then there is *Kokkie*, the cook. She arrives each morning carrying a large enamel bowl resting in a bird's-nest *slendang* on her head. It is overflowing with food, bought at the local *pasar*, or market. There is always something exciting to see in Kokkie's bowl. Today there is a live white-feathered chicken, its head dangling over the side of the bowl, its feet tied together with raffia.

There is always fresh fish or kapitting (crab) with its claws also tied together with raffia. There may be sweet tiny *pisang* (bananas) called *pisang soesoe*, or the giant ones, *pisang radjah*, which kokkie uses for banana fritters.

There are tiny red and green peppers, which Pappie has for a snack with his drink in the early evening. They are called *tjabe*, and they are exceedingly hot. Pappie munches away at them as if they are salted peanuts! We know not to touch them, as even handling them can have disastrous effects. I remember the day I disobeyed and tried a tjabe. The fire in my mouth was so hot, so appalling, that I will never try them again. But that day, alas! Having spat out the tiny piece, I still had the juice on my fingers and rubbed my eye. It left me crying and panicking with pain, streaming eyes, and an unimaginable burning sensation, never to be forgotten!

Our garden has a high wall all around it, and atop the wall are shards of green glass imbedded in the concrete to deter burglars. The garden itself is large and exciting. There is an very large old *waringing* tree. The locals call these holy trees. A mysterious creeper climbs up and into the tangled, dipping branches. It bears enormous purple flowers the shape of a Dutchman's pipe, which hang freely in the canopy. We have been told to keep away from the tree. The tree is so large that it houses a host of creatures. There are poisonous creepy-crawlies, snakes, and flea-ridden fruit bats. But this is all the more reason for me to go ferreting round! I am always hoping for a deliciously dangerous encounter with a green-eyed snake. I can *feel* the eyes of the snake following me around, and part of me wants to run, but mostly I want to see.

There are tiny scarlet flower peckers sipping nectar from the purple Dutchman's-pipe flowers. A *tokeh*, a large wall climbing lizard who calls his own name and booms his sonorous 'Tokeh … tokeh … tokeh …' all through the evening. The T-T-T-T sounds hard and loud. I can never listen without stopping whatever I am doing and then counting. One …two … three … If a tokeh calls seven times in a row, I may have a wish. There are so many tokehs on this island that I am kept counting throughout the evening.

The servants weave tiny grass offerings, each embellished with a fresh flower and together with a small basket of cooked rice. They leave these gifts each dawn at the foot of the tree, to appease the spirits that live in the tree. White cloths are tied round the tree, smeared with sulphur-yellow ointment called *boreh*. Sometimes a tiny glass jar with boreh will be presented on a banana leaf with a pretty orchid. Whatever the gift, it is always artistically presented and intended to please.

I am constantly getting into trouble for picking up giant stag beetles, tiny delicate *tjitjak* (wall-climbing lizards), the vicious red gran-gran ants, or small snakes, but it is my chief delight! Picking up any one of these creatures can result in a painful bite and infection, but I cannot help myself, and even the servants tell me off.

There are ancient *angrek*, or orchids, growing in the crown of the tree. An orchid has to be forty years old before it starts flowering, and my orchid flowers most of the year, so it must be very old.

The *put*—or well—is also within the confines of our garden. It is surrounded by a six-foot whitewashed wall; a narrow gap without a door gives entry to the washing area. This place is strictly out of bounds for us children. There are two good reasons. It is a dangerous place, as the well is deep and full of water. But more importantly, it is the private mandi for the servants. We know that this is the place where they strip and haul up the *gajoeng* (the bucket) brimming with cool water. We all wash like that, throwing the cold water over our bodies. The first bucketful is cold and accompanied with lots of noises. The Indonesians are very clean people and often mandi several times a day. They use a tin of soft green soap, their monthly ration as part of their wages.

Nicolette, Frank, and I try to sneak up on them when we hear the noise coming from the mandi. Screams and yells, '*Ajo nonnie—ajo sinjo!*' (Go away girl, go away boy!) follow us as we hastily scarper. But no matter, as we shall risk another peep another day, until the servants pluck up courage and report our misdemeanours to Mammie.

Not far from the quayside is an old Dutch fort, Fort Rotterdam. During the war years this place held several thousands of Dutch women and children imprisoned, but now the big wooden gates stand wide open. The Portuguese first built this as a fortified outpost in 1545. The Dutch captured it in 1608.

The gardens within the walls are verdant, and tall palm trees fringe the tops of the whitewashed stone walls. The shape of the fort is like a turtle facing the city with its tail pointing towards the sea. Outside the gates are the *kromos* (sellers) with their *pikolans* (yokes with baskets dangling from each side). The pikolans are piled high with things to buy and things to eat.

We are not allowed to buy any of the tempting goodies, as most are prepared with river water. The river, or *kali*, is used for everything. The women use the kali for doing their laundry, and it is perfectly acceptable to squat and poo in the same river. Ice-lollies are made with river water, and vegetables are washed in it.

The only kromo that is welcome to sell his wares to us is the *katjang* (peanut) kromo. We hear him long before we see him. He tinkles his bell and monotonously calls, 'Katja-a-a-a-ang, katja-a-a-a-ang, katjang goreng.' When the katjang kromo is beckoned, he gently puts down his pikolan with the two charcoal burners and prepares the fried peanuts while we watch. He then hands each of us a small cone-shaped piece of newspaper piled high with hot peanuts. It is a special, simple treat, and we enjoy the warm packet in our fingers. We rub each katjang to remove its oily skin before we eat it.

Sometimes the kromos come to buy our empty tins. Our Blue Band margarine comes in an enormous tin, with a cheerful blue band painted around it. The margarine is very salty, to preserve it in this very hot climate, and kokkie spends a long time squeezing it under the running tap to remove the surplus salt before it is ready for consumption.

Every tin or glass jar is washed and kept for recycling. Once a month the kromo arrives, squatting patiently on the tiled veranda floor while *tjawarren* (bargaining) the right price with Mammie. The tins will be recycled into cooking utensils, toys, or trinkets. The kromo does the rounds from one European home to the next. Nothing is wasted. His tins are tied in bundles and neatly stacked in the baskets hanging from his shoulders. Sometimes he carries so many tins that it is hard to see the man beneath them. A few tins are loosely tied together, and with each step the soft music created from the tins clanging together announces the coming of the tin kromo.

Another kromo who visits our home is the egg lady. She practises the same gentle routine of bargaining for the right price. No one is ever in a hurry. Mammie sits in her rattan chair on the veranda with two large enamel pans, one of which is filled with water by her feet. Each egg is gently lowered into the water, while we sit around, watching and waiting to see whether the egg will lie on the floor of the bowl. If it points upwards or, worse still, floats to the surface, we all shout in unison, *'Boesoek!'*—which, of course, means it is rotten or addled. But the egg lady does not remove the rotten egg; she puts it back in her basket to try her next customer.

Learning To Play

There is a newcomer to our household. Katjong is the odd-job man. He can turn his hand to anything and is at the beck and call of all the other servants. He will help Kokkie fill up her range of charcoal burners and help the *kebon* (gardener) rake the paths every afternoon. He will clean our shoes, fetch and carry, and wash the car under supervision of the chauffeur. He also keeps a about 4 or 5 tiny cages woven from grasses in which he keeps his *djankriks* (crickets).

The djankriks are kept for amusement and taken out of their cages to fight each other. Katjong irritates and incites them with a special grass blade. We all squat around the djankriks, shouting encouragement while the tiny creatures box and fight each other till one is too exhausted to go on.

Katjong feeds the djankriks on tiny pieces of the fiery-hot red peppers from the kitchens. This, he says, is to get them into a fighting mood.

Both Djongos and Katjong are masters at entertaining the children. While we sit and watch, Djongos will carve us carts with wheels on axles of slivers of bamboo. The carts are carved from the big, carrot-shaped, black-skinned radishes called *grobak*. The black skin is removed, and small pieces of artwork appear from his skilful hands. We receive the small homemade toys with big sighs of pleasure.

At other times, the pair will spend an afternoon making us windmills. Small squares of paper, pins, and two bamboo sticks in the shape of a cross will soon become whizzing windmills that keep us entertained for days.

Best of all is kite time. Our kites are not big, but they are made for fighting. To make our kites, Djongos gathers together colourful paper, bamboo sticks, string, and a homemade glue made from *ketan*, the glutinous rice used for sweetmeats. The kites have long colourful tails and smiling faces. But best of all is the glass cord, which forms the three meters of string nearest the kite. Pieces of glass are pounded with a stone till resembling coarse powder, which is then glued to the string. When dried, it becomes a formidable weapon for the kite players. The secret with kite fights is to cross someone else's kite string. If you angle at just the right place, it cuts the string of the opponent's kite. Oh, what victory to see the other kite fall from the sky. But Djongos is always available to mend a disgraced kite.

Knuckles is another game we play with great enthusiasm. Pappie tells us that when he was a boy, the game was played with real knuckles. His real knuckles were made of the bony joints of a monkey's hand. Mine are made from shiny brass, and Djongos teases me, saying that I spend more time polishing the knuckles than playing them.

Our small ball is home-made from local latex. Latex trees grow everywhere on the island, and every child living in the tropics knows that a small cut in the bark of the tree will produce the white, sticky fluid that, when collected and its thin thread wound round and round, will produce a very bouncy ball. This game can be played by one person only as I do most of the time. If it is shared by others we take it in turn. The aim of this game is about great dexterity of the hand, as each knuckle has to be turned to the show same side of each knuckle between the bouncing of the ball and then the catching of the ball with the other hand. My knuckles are kept in a pink gingham bag with a silk drawstring. I am not much good at the game but will spend hours practising, as I love the sound of the knuckles dropping on the tiled floor.

Djongos has also made me a top. It is made from *djatti* wood (teak) and has a nail driven in the bottom end. The djatti has been soaked for days in *assem* water, made from the leaves of the tamarind tree in our garden. This helps to harden the wood and so protects it from chipping. The nail is sharpened and the lovely dark wood buffed up. Three coloured crayons to draw a coloured band, and my top is complete. The secret is to wind the string as neatly as possible round the top. A quick twist of the wrist will start the top spinning.

I do not really like the top fights. The aim is to see who can splinter the other tops or even put them out of action. I treasure my top and enjoy watching the coloured bands blur as the top spins faster and faster. I'll leave the boys to have their contests.

Makassar, 1946

We are having our first portrait taken. It is being taken especially to send to Mammie's family in Holland. This we know is the country of our queen, Wilhelmina. It is where Oma and Opa live and lots of aunts and uncles. We have no idea what any of those people look like. If we did have any pictures of them before the war, we abandoned them all at some time during the many moves we made from one camp to another.

My hair has been washed with soft green soap, and I am wearing my best frock of blue cotton with an embroidered band of red and white flowers across my chest. Nicolette wears a pretty red and white striped dress. Frank wears white. Boys in the tropics only ever wear white, as do the men.

We enter the photographer's shop and behind the glass cabinets we see a display of pictures: babies on goatskin rugs and lots of children with shining faces and neatly combed hair. There are pictures of families looking smart and spruced up, teenage girls with innocent smiles, and boys with slicked hair, nothing out of place.

The Chinese man, his hair plaited into a long, thin, black plait, tells us where to sit and what not to do. He arranges his huge black camera on a tripod and fusses over the seating, but finally he has us sitting exactly how he likes it. I feel oh-so shy. I have been told to sit *very* still and smile. It is very hard to concentrate on both at the same time. But we dare not do anything other than what we are told. This is a very special place and a great occasion for us. We have never seen a photograph of ourselves. The small man puts his head under a cloth. 'Are you ready?' he asks. 'Yes? Don't move!' and *click*.

The pictures around us are most likely the first pictures taken of grandchildren living in the Far East to be sent to curious omas and opas in Europe.

Some children, like my brother Frank, have never been seen by any member of the family. These pictures will be the first taken since the Japanese occupation and the end of war.

It is October 1946 It has been 10 months since we were re-united as a family. Many changes have happened since then, but the biggest change to our family is about to happen. We have been told that we are going to have a new brother or sister,

Today the day has come that mammie is taken to the Stella Maris Hospital. The following day we are shown our new sister, Heleen. She is so very tiny and very white with little fluffs of blond hair. She sleeps peacefully in the wooden hospital cot.

As for me, I am much more interested in the nurses in their smart, starched, white dresses and aprons, their large caps, and the lovely smell of antiseptic fluid that pervades the air. I know instantly that when I grow up I want to be a nurse too.

We have got another servant. She is the *baboe tjoetie*, or laundry maid. With all the extra nappies and clothing for four children, Tjoetie will be kept busy.

All laundry is washed by hand in cold water. A large cardboard tin of soft green soap is at hand, and the laundry is pummelled on the corrugated wooden washing board. It is rinsed in giant tin tubs and hung, dripping, on the lines.

A special area of the garden is kept for the laundry, and we are not allowed on the grassy bit, where all whites are laid neatly on the grass. The grass will help it bleach whiter than white. In this hot climate the laundry is dry in less than an hour.

Tjoetie has three irons. Each is heated on a charcoal fire. Tjoetie rubs the hot surface of the little iron on an old towel before using it, to ensure no sooty bits are left, which might spoil the clothes. It is hot work, and Tjoetie takes all day just dealing with the laundry.

The giant linen cupboard has many shelves and when the doors are opened, a wonderful perfume permeates the air. Tjoeti will have learned all she knows about how to keep the laundry looking and smelling at its very best from her own mother. So when Tjoetie has finished for the day, she goes into the garden to collect the small, white, highly scented flowers of the jasmine plant, which we call *melatti*, into a small basket. Sitting cross-legged on the floor, she peacefully spends a few hours stringing the tiny flowers on cotton threads. They are then hung across the many shelves to scent the white linen. Time is this hot climate has little meaning. Being peacefull while stringing the melatti is all part of this days

All our clothes are made from cotton, as that is all that is available here; we do not know about wool and modern material have not reached these shores yet.

In the tropics we all keep siestas. We eat a large rice meal with many separate little dishes of fish, or meat, or vegetables at lunchtime. It is called a rijsttafel and is an invention of the Dutch colonials, as the locals eat very much simpler meals.

After eating such a large meal, we simply have to have a rest, as it is the hottest time of the day. We are under strict orders not to make a noise. We children do not sleep, of course, but the adults do. So we whisper but on the whole are too afraid of Mammie's rule of rules.

Kokkie cooks us special dishes, which she brings to our bedroom in the late afternoon, reminding us to be quiet and not so much as squeak. She knows exactly the sort of dishes we like: pisang goreng, or banana fritters, and sometimes a plateful of pieces of sugar cane, which we suck till all the juices are gone.

Very occasionally she bakes a spek cake. The Dutch word *spek* means bacon. The cake resembles streaky bacon as it is cooked in seven or eight separate layers of light- and dark-coloured spicy mix. It takes a very experienced cook and a great deal of time to bake this cake. It is so rich that we only get a thin sliver of cake at a time. It tastes of ground cloves and cinnamon and cardamom and is the best thing she cooks.

Mammie will for the rest of our lives worry about our eating habits, forever trying to make us eat more and more. She is always trying to fatten us up! She longs for the European food that she has not tasted for so many years. One of the Dutch specialties she longs for is strawberries. We, of course, have never tasted strawberries, so she gets Kokkie to prepare us a plate of make-believe strawberries by slicing tomatoes and sprinkling them with sugar! I am far too timid to tell her I prefer my tomatoes with salt and pepper, so I struggle through a large plateful again and again.

At last the siesta comes to an end, and we take turns to go to the mandi to sluice ourselves with ice-cold water from the tub. The mandi room is big and dark and slippery. It is green with algae. It has a large concrete tub in the corner, with a bamboo chute delivering a constant trickle of water. I hate going into the mandi by myself, as I imagine the corners to be full of monsters looking at me. I can also see a hole to the outside world, where the water pipe enters the mandi.

My monster squeezes through the little hole and then slithers into the tub, waiting for small people, which it eats—hair, teeth, nails, and bones—all in one big mouthful!

When I return to my room, freshly laundered and ironed clothes have been laid on my bed by Tjoetie. She decides what I wear, and it does not occur to me to question her choice. It is a big joke in the family that Hanneke's clean clothes will be smudged and grubby in less than an hour.

Once dressed, I go straight back to my beloved tree, crawling round on all fours as I try to catch every creepy-crawly. I am quite oblivious of how I look. In contrast, Nicolette always looks clean and well groomed. She keeps her frocks so clean that she can wear them for more than one day. Alas, this pattern will remain for the rest of our lives.

The adults have a cup of tea while we have a glass of *djeroek*, freshly squeezed orange juice with water. But today Kokkie has made assem syrup, a concentrated syrup from tamarind beans that we mix with water. It is a refreshing drink, which we have in large quantities.

Occasionally the servants have their friends round for a visit. I enjoy these visits as I sit on the tiled floor of the blakan. The blakan is the part of our home that houses the servants, the kitchens, and laundry room; it is connected to the house by a covered walkway. Kokkie does her cooking outside on charcoal burners, and this is where the servants all relax and socialize.

The visitors arrive at the gate and courteously greet my parents with their hands together, touching their faces. 'Pagi, Toean ... Njonja.'

(Afternoon, Mr ... Mrs.) Visitors always arrive with gifts for us, as is their custom. Sometimes there are sweetmeats wrapped in banana leaves. Other times there will be a giant coconut. Djongos will set to with his big knife to chop away the green, shiny husk before slicing the top off. The nuts are always young, freshly picked, and brimming with milk. Kokkie will give us a glass of assem syrup topped up with coconut milk and paper-thin slices of sweet young nut. Occasionally a special surprise emerges as Djongos slices the top—a baby coconut inside. It tastes like nothing else in the world.

These kind people do not mind if I sit with them and listen to their abundant laughter and their interesting stories. They will often include me in their conversation and their relaxed joviality. No one ever reminds me that I should not really be there.

The light quickly changes at this time of the day, and so do the sounds. The djankriks start up their orchestra, and we hear the kromos announcing their wares.

Sometimes Mammie decides to take us to buy pieces of colourful material for new frocks. She is a wonderful seamstress and makes all our clothes on her Singer treadle machine.

If the chauffeur is not around to take us in the car, we get Djongos to get us two *betjaks*. A betjak is a two-seater pushbike taxi. A canopy separates the driver and his passengers and keeps them out of the sun. We all pile into the betjaks and travel to the main street of Makassar just behind the harbour walls.

Inside the little *tokos* (shops), enormous fans are suspended from the ceiling and drone out their monotonous whirring sound. The Chinese shopkeeper immediately appears and offers us sweets and green tea while we wait. Mammie asks him to bring out roll after roll, exclaiming time and again, '*Adoe*—too expensive. But in the end she decides on some pretty print for two dresses, one for Nicolette and one for me. It never occurs to us to question her choice. The cloth is wrapped in brown paper and tied with a piece of string. (This will be carefully unpicked later and kept for reuse in the drawer in the desk.) It takes a long time to get the parcel exactly right, but finally the smiling shopkeeper hands the parcel to Nicolette to carry.

When we emerge from the toko only thirty minutes later, darkness has descended. In the tropics darkness comes swiftly. Everywhere the oil lamps are lit, and the smell of paraffin oil permeates the air. Larongs (flying ants) and mosquitoes gather round the lights, and the soft night sounds begin.

Tokehs boom out their voices, and tjitjaks, very small wall climbing house lizards, gather round the lights to begin their night hunting of mosquitoes. The frogs croak in the numerous ditches surrounding each house, which carry away the unthinkable as well as the monsoon rains.

The *slokans*, or ditches, are smelly but nevertheless fascinating places to watch the small, brightly coloured blue and scarlet kapitting (land crabs). These live in small holes along the steep sides of the slokan. I know if I am patient and sit very quietly, the shy crabs will eventually venture out from their homes. They will scuttle sideways in search of food, but the slightest movement will see them shoot back to the safety of their little round doorways.

I have tried unsuccessfully to catch them. Small as they are, they are so much faster than I will ever be. I have visions of catching enough to present to kokkie.

She sometimes comes back from the early morning market with live sea crabs, their mighty claws tied together with a piece of raffia. Kokkie boils them in a pan of bubbling water, and they quickly turn bright red from the drab grey. To make quite sure the crabs are fresh, she dips a silver spoon into the water. If the silver turns black, the crab is poisonous and not fit to eat.

Our First School

We are starting school in Makassar! Because of the heat in the tropics, school starts at seven in the morning and finishes at midday. Nicolette and I are very excited when we are walked, under supervision of Djongos, to our first school. It is a Roman Catholic school, run by nuns.

The nuns look wonderful in their voluminous, crisp, white habits. Their headdresses are so enormous and starched that only by looking at them from the front can I see their faces. Whispered rumours say that they have no hair, as it is shaved off as part of their commitment to Jesus. Their hands invariably are folded together. They make no unexpected movements, and they speak gently, never raising their voices. They wear white soft-soled shoes, and when they walk, all that can be heard is the swish, swish, swish of their starched habits. The only adornment against the white habit is the long chain with the cross of dark wood and the silver figure of Jesus.

The nuns are kind but very strict, and discipline is an important part of school life.

These same women were at the heart of our survival in the camps. They took on care of the sick and dying in the hospitals. With no family or children of their own to care for, they directed their energies at spiritually leading the women and children. They led the illicit prayer groups, knowing all the familiar hymns—but most of all they kept hope in a future burning in the hearts of the captives. Their courage in defending their patients against all odds from the wrath of the Nippon became legendary.

Each morning, in complete silence, we line up in the shady verandas of the convent, and in a long crocodile, walking hand in hand with our neighbours, we are taken to the convent church in the centre of the complex. As we enter the large, ornate church, on the right hand side, just inside the massive doors, there is a small stone font set into the wall. Each child dips her fingers into the water and crosses herself. We have little idea what this is for, but like all children around the world, we follow the leader; it is part of the discipline.

It is only some weeks later that Mammie questions us about it and tells us that as Protestants we must not do such Catholic things. But we, of course, continue to cross ourselves, so as not to stand out among our friends. There are candles and incense too, and the smell inside the church is wonderful.

There are no exercise books yet, but we all possess our own slates, with wooden surrounds and a small hole in the top with a piece of string to keep the slate pencil in place. Small pieces of cloth to wipe the slates clean and we have all we need for our lessons.

There are so many children wanting to learn that the school overflows its classrooms to outside. My classroom is beneath a huge waringing tree. A three-legged blackboard stands facing us. Our ages vary by two or three years. There are children much older than myself in my class who have had no education at all in the long years of captivity. We sit on long wooden benches, balancing our slates on our knees. But the discomfort of it does not bother anyone. After the years of boredom without education, everyone is excited with all that is being offered us.

Each child is like a sponge and has a capacity to absorb information ad infinitum. It takes me no time at all to learn to read, sharing the dog-eared little books with two other friends. There are songs and sums and two languages to cope with. At the end of our school day, it is storytelling time from a book called *Grimm's Fairy Tales* or another called *Javanese Fairy Tales*. Both our cultures are important to us, and we embrace both as our own.

Djongos is patiently waiting for us outside the convent gates at midday, and we walk back home discussing everything with him that has happened to us that day.

A Parcel From Holland

A parcel from Holland has arrived. We all gather round and admire it, as it has a number of stamps on it with pictures of our queen. We have endlessly talked about Queen Wilhelmina, her daughter Princess Juliana, and her granddaughters. But this is the very first time we have seen a picture of her. Some patriotic women carried clandestine pictures of our queen around with them throughout the war years. But never before has her portrait been openly displayed.

This is also the first time we are receiving presents that have been bought especially for each of us. All through the camp years, birthdays passed with few real surprises. The Dutch are good at birthdays. Everyone knows everyone's birthday. It would be unthinkable to forget your neighbours' birthdays or their children's. In the camps, birthdays were a good excuse to relieve the boredom, and even the tiniest gift was better than nothing. A homemade picture, a poem, a few flowers, half an egg, or a banana bought at great risk through the gedekking would be very acceptable gifts.

The little khaki coloured army mirror Pappie gave me on our first reunion was the first real gift I ever received.

This box, however, contains real presents, chosen for children. There is—wonder of wonders!—a doll for me, wrapped in brown paper. She has a papier mâché face, rather squashed and ugly. But to me she is just beautiful. Her brown hair is painted onto her skull. Her body is made from cloth and rather lumpy; her socks and shoes are papier mâché and painted also. She wears clothes that can be taken off and put on again. One of her curious bits of clothing is a blue flower-printed cap, tied under her chin with silk ribbon. I have never before seen anyone, other than the nuns, wearing hats. I call her Loesje, and she never leaves my arms from that day onwards. I have entered a new phase of my life, as here is someone I have to take care of.

That is not all! Another brown-wrapped parcel contains a big box labelled Post Office. Inside there are sheets of tiny stamps separated by perforations. There is a metal box with pad and ink and a rubber stamp that says Post Kantoor (Post Office in Dutch). There are three pads of writing paper, two small pencils, a rubber, envelopes, and lined paper. There are also some small squares of white card, rubber bands, and a pencil sharpener. Until now I have never heard of a post office, but it takes no time at all to get the hang of becoming a postmistress—although I do remember with shame my stinginess with my precious stamps and paper!

This wonderful parcel has come from Mammie's younger sister, Lena, in Holland. Will she ever realize what her gifts and generosity mean to these small people?

Our horizons are growing with each day. New vistas are opening up, and we are learning to accept and enjoy another world, one beyond the confines of our own limited early life.

New Horizons, 1947

We are going on a journey! We have heard our parents talk about our Dutch family, and we are now going to see them.

Our other grandparent have died during the war and are buried in the small mountainous town in mid Java called Salatiga. Our grandmother, Koosje Hoorn Levasier, died in 1944. As she was a diabetic, the inadequate food supply during the war did not support the elderly lady. Our grandfather, Franciscus Hoorn, died not long after peace was declared. Neither went into a camp.

One of the reasons we went into camps was that at the beginning of the war it was thought to be the safest option for European families. We went in voluntarily, thinking it was the right decision to make.

The Red Cross has informed us that all of the Dutch family has survived. But the last winter of the war in Europe has been truly horrific. People have been surviving on a diet of tulip bulbs, and many of the beautiful parkland trees throughout the country have been cut down to provide fuel during the last bitter winter months. We have no concept of what winter is, but we are going to arrive during the winter, and have been promised snow!

It is hard for us to understand the word *snow*. I have been told it is white and cold and can melt. Our own concept of cold is going into the mountain regions to 'get a cold nose', an expression used by all Europeans to explain a few days respite from the sticky heat in the lowlands.

An extra cardigan to wear in the cool of the evening is all we would need. A thin cotton bed cover at night would be sufficient to deal with our kind of 'cold'.

However, we shall need coats and winter woollies and stockings when we go to Europe. Even the words *coat* and *stocking* are an unknown quantity to us. Mammie says she will feel like a coat hanger!

A beautiful ship called N.V. *Johan van Oldenbarnnveld* is docked at Jakarta's harbour, Tantjoeng Priok. This pre-war passenger ship was turned into a troop ship throughout the war, and it will now carry some of the refugee families returning to Holland for the first time since peace was declared. The journey will take four weeks.

The ship is full of wonderful surprises! The foods we are served are a daily journey of discovery, and a whole host of new tastes are being added to our simple palates. There is cheese and fresh milk. The only milk we've known is the dried variety that comes from a tall, round tin. It is measured carefully with a spoon and mixed most vigorously in a jug before it is ready for consumption. If the stirring has not been vigorous enough, crunchy bits of dried milk remain in my mouth and need to be worked at with my tongue. It is not a nice sensation!

There are apples—big, red, and sweet. They come from Australia. The bread is soft and white, and there is always enough to satisfy a hungry child. There are jams made of fruits we do not know and something called *appelstroop*, a brown, gooey, tart apple spread. There is peanut butter and slices of thin smoked horsemeat. We eat our first potatoes and sauerkraut. I have never eaten cheese before, and my first taste of this savoury food is a most welcome addition to my fast-growing range of new tastes.

Nicolette is not well, and she is kept in sickbay for most of the journey. The doctors and nurses look very smart in their crisp white uniforms, their soft white shoes, and big starched headdresses. It is pleurisy that Nicolette has—she is very ill indeed! Nicolette is my best friend, and I am very worried about her, as the adults speak about her in whispers. They have allowed me to visit the ward once only, and I am shocked to see her white, thin face.

After two weeks at sea, we come to the Suez Canal. Everyone talks about the man who built the canal; a giant statue of Ferdinand de Lesseps stands on the banks of the canal. I have never before seen a statue, and this one makes a deep impression.

On both sides of the canal we see desert, just mile after mile of grey sand. There are people wearing long robes and riding camels or donkeys on the banks of the canal. I am becoming aware of new cultures, different people, and another climate.

My life is suddenly overflowing with new horizons. This is where East meets West, and the passengers begin to feel excited at the prospect of reaching home.

On arrival at the town of Suez, we are all taken by train to an encampment called Ataka. The journey in the Desert Express is not very glamorous, as there is standing room only in what looks like a cattle train. But everyone is so excited that no one complains at this basic transportation. We are going to be fitted out by the Red Cross into our European clothing.

When we arrive, we are offered orange squash and sweet biscuits and are seated at small tables with pretty cloths and rattan chairs. The ceiling is festooned with bunting and hundreds of small Dutch tricolour flags. There are orange flags to remind us of the royal family of the House of Orange.

There is a play area for children, with equipment that none of us could ever have dreamt of: little wooden seesaws, a sandpit overflowing with cups and shapes, a box full of building blocks, a box full of dolls and another with dolls' clothes. We have never seen so many toys. There is no squabbling or shouting; we are too overwhelmed by such plenty.

After a while we are taken to another building, and there on long trestle tables are piles and piles of neatly folded clothes and shoes in every shape and size imaginable. After a great deal of fitting and discussion, we come away with cardboard boxes piled high with clothes to keep us warm in the coldest of weathers.

Some of the garments are very strange indeed. I have been given three long pink-ribbed vests. On the sides are stitched white cotton strips with buttons at five-centimetre intervals. Flesh coloured stockings with buttonholed elastic sewn into the sides will team up with the pink vest buttons to hold them in place.

There are mittens held together and tied to the little loop inside the back of my navy wool jacket. A little black cap completes the outfit. None of the clothes are new, and they smell of mothballs.

It is still far too hot to be wearing so many layers of clothes, so we hang them in the cabin cupboard for the time being. Several times a day I go and look at them, fingering the unfamiliar cloth.

My horizon widens yet again with new place names. There is Gibraltar and then the Bay of Biscay. The captain tells us over the tannoy to look on the starboard side, as large schools of flying fish are giving us the performance of their lives. Their silvery bodies leap high into the air, and indeed they appear to be flying as they move across the surface of the water for quite a distance.

But the waters are very rough in the bay, and I am very sick, along with almost everyone else.

Very soon it is time for us to be putting on our winter clothes. I feel very smart and oh-so proud to be going to Holland. There is a festive mood on board. Most people are returning to their homeland, which they left more than eight years earlier. Most of us children have never met our Dutch relatives before, let alone been in Europe.

Mammie went out to the East Indies in 1937 to marry the man of her dreams, so it is nine years since she last saw her parents, brother, and sister.

Holland

The great ship's funnel is hooting a celebratory welcome as we enter the harbour of Rotterdam. Our grandfather, Gerlof Aergelo, or Opa, as we will call him, together with Mammie's sister, Lena, are waiting for us at the draughty dockyard.

The little luggage we have with us is taken onto the train, and once again I am overwhelmed with so many new impressions. There seem to be houses everywhere, closely packed together, and so many people on bicycles, all wrapped up against the biting wind. And then there is the snow! I am finally seeing this cold, white stuff that covers everything, including the roofs on the tall houses.

We have never seen houses of more than one story. But these houses have windows reaching up into the sky, and we have yet to learn that Dutch houses have stairs.

Well, at last we arrive in the little ancient town of Deventer, with its mighty medieval church beside the river IJssel. The home of our grandparents is on the 2de Pauwelandstraat, Number 31. It is a three-story corner house with a small garden at the front and rear.

Our grandmother, or Oma, as we call her, is a tiny lady of no more than five feet high. Her cheeks are rosy, and she has a tiny grey bun at the back of her head. She wears round pebble glasses, and she smiles and smiles, quite unnerved by the invasion of six extra people into her home for the next six months. She is so lovely that I feel instantly at home here.

Opa is a studious man, full of wisdom and gentleness; he is an old soldier. For him, things have to be orderly and done in exactly the right way. Opa goes to the library each week. I love going with him as he moves from section to section, collecting his full allocation of seven books each week. I soon learn that speaking in the library is strictly taboo—even whispering is frowned upon. I also learn that if I want to come with him I have to be patient while he leafs through book after book before adding it to his growing pile. But I am no stranger to being patient, as the camp years taught me to be self-contained, so I amuse myself with watching young and old quietly looking through books.

Opa has got me my own library ticket, and when he has collected his own pile, we move to the children's section, where paradise awaits me. Having been deprived all my young life of knowledge, books will always be a comfort to me no matter where I am in the world. Opa generously treats my time for choosing my books in the way that he expected me to treat his time, with patience. Nothing is ever hurried when I am with Opa.

We soon learn to give Opa space and respect and quiet when he reads his books. The same applies when he listens to the one o'clock and six o clock news on his large brown Bakelite radio. Woe betide if we dare as much as whisper when Opa is listening to the news. He raises his finger in warning when he ceremoniously turns the knob on the radio just one minute before the great clock booms its hour. It gives him enough time to remove the large silver watch on its silver chain from inside his jacket pocket, in readiness to adjust its hour dial to the precise second when the clock sounds.

He is a man full of interesting stories gleaned from his travel books, autobiographies, history books, and newspapers. In these days without the visual aid of television, his general knowledge is unsurpassed. Numerous times a day he will come out with quotations in either French or Latin. He will then patiently help us translate them, giving us generous credit when we come close to an understanding.

Oma quietly spends most of the day preparing food, shopping in the market or local stores. It is quite remarkable how unfazed this tiny lady is by cooking and cleaning and washing for eight people every day. Her kitchen has a battery of paraffin burners for cooking. There is no hot water or bathroom.

Our weekly bath is on the kitchen floor in a tin tub. Opa goes off to the local bathhouse for his weekly scrub. He spends three mornings a week at the barber's for a shave.

The hall in the house has black and white marble tiles on the floor, and the grandfather clock, with its pear-shaped weights, softly ticks life into this dark and cold part of the house.

There is no heating other than the giant stove in the drawing room and the paraffin stove in the kitchen. The one in the drawing room is fed mostly with coal, but next to it stands a big basket piled high with brown, crumbly blocks of peat. The stove is kept going in the night with the peat, ensuring a gentle, constant heat.

The floors in the bedrooms are covered in cold, worn linoleum. During the long winter months we wake up many mornings to opaque and frosted windows. Jack Frost creates a riot of artistic frost flowers upon the glass of the windows during the night, much to my delight. A porcelain potty underneath my bed saves a trip downstairs in the middle of the night.

Opa smokes cigars. He has a large, flat balsam-wood box full of them. They are laid out in a pretty pattern on the scarlet silk lining, a big cigar in the centre and the smaller ones fanlike towards the edges. Each cigar has a pretty coloured band round the top, and I love watching Opa ceremoniously remove the band and present me with it. He then produces a thin blue-covered exercise book and shows me how to glue the cigar band on the first page. He promises me that if I am a good girl he will me give a band every time he starts a new cigar.

Not every cigar Opa smokes is finished in one go. Some are so big that he will relight them several days running. Many Dutch men smoke cigars, so there are other sources for me to collect my cigar bands from. There is even a little song that I learn to sing, to encourage other cigar-smoking men to part with their cigar bands. Before long, my first collection grows into a colourful bookful.

When I go shyly up to the cigar-smoking gentlemen in the barbershop to ask if I may have their cigar bands, they never part with them without first asking and fully expecting me to sing the song first.

We watch avidly when Opa goes through the elaborate ritual of starting a new cigar. His pocketknife has a special blade to cut off the end bit of the cigar. First the band comes off and is handed to me and admired by all. Then the knife comes out, the right blade is chosen, and under our watchful eyes, the bit is sliced off. He loves the attention he gets when the ceremony starts. We all smile with relief when he inhales the first lungful and one of us is offered the burning match to blow out.

Sometimes Opa will keep us mesmerized by blowing smoke rings for us. The house smells of sweet cigar smoke, but Oma cleans the big glass ashtray twice a day and opens the windows, whatever the weather, to blow fresh air right through the house.

During the summer months, the pretty garden is like an extension to the house. It is not exactly child friendly, but no matter, we are content to play our games with neighbourhood friends in the street or be invited to neighbours' gardens.

There are some wonderful trees in Oma's garden that we have never heard of before. There is a lilac tree—and intriguingly, half the tree produces fragrant, snow-white trusses, while the other half has mauve flowers. It is a miracle tree, and Oma is very proud of it.

There is also an ornamental cherry tree. Very early in spring it produces pink rosebud-like flowers all along its bare branches. Each flower is no larger than my fingernail and a creation of perfection.

At the bottom of the garden grows a row of raspberry canes. Great is the excitement the day when we may pick the first fruits! This is my earliest awareness of the different flowers in different continents and climates.

There are no restrictions in this land on what we may or may not pick or which creatures we may handle. There are no poisonous beetles or spiders or snakes lurking in the branches of trees. This is a straightforward land.

There are, however, some restrictions that are far more baffling to a small girl. I have a new friend called Toke. She is blonde, and vivacious, and pretty, and a good friend. Mammie calls me one day and explains it is better if I do not get too friendly with Toke, as it has come to her ear that Toke is a Catholic. I am not to go into her home again. 'Remember, she is different.'

No one is able to answer my questions as to why that should be bad for me. Toke's mother is kind and gentle and generous. I will from now on be careful not to mention Toke's name again, but in my first act of wilful rebellion, I keep Toke as my friend, and I ponder why God should differentiate between Protestants and Catholics.

The matter of God has been part of my thinking since I was baptized in the Dutch Reformed Berg Kerk (Berg kerk means Church on the mountain; in the low land of Holland the tiny incline this church is situated on is considered a mountain; hence the name Mountain church!)

All of us children (except Nicolette, who was baptized on Java before the war) are baptized on 28 September 1947. A brand-new dress of green wool, a cross on my forehead, and I am told that God has called me by my name. So, who is this mysterious God? I know about Jesus and his birth in a stable. I know about the flight to Egypt and many more wonderful stories. But God remains an enigma to me for many years to come.

Nicolette has never really recovered from her illness at sea, so she was eventually admitted to the local Hospital, but finally been allowed to return home from the I have not been allowed to see her more than once, as hospitals are no places for children.

How wonderful to be reunited with this sibling who has been my best friend, mentor, protector, and confidante. She looks a pale shadow of her former self, but no matter. She is alive, and my nightmares about losing her are gone.

No one has thought to talk to the children about Nicolette's long absence. All I know about her condition is what I have gleaned from gloomy conversations held in hushed voices. I am equally certain Nicolette herself has been told little or nothing about her illness.

Nicolette is shy and quiet. In the school grounds she can often be found standing with her back against the wall, not joining in the games, just watching the noisy crowd.

School in Holland is very different from the open-air school on Java or the Roman Catholic school we attended on Celebes. Here we each just have a slate, and the only books we have are those we share with the rest of the class. But now we have been given real pencils, and Opa has spent an afternoon sharpening his penknife and putting sharp ends on the pencils. Then there is real paper and thin, blue exercise books. We each have a wooden pencil box, which holds far more than mere pencils: a pen and a selection of shiny new nibs, a rubber, marbles, and a piece of cloth to clean the nibs with.

There are proper reading books and wonderful charts mounted on the flaking walls. The letters of the alphabet cover one chart. Each letter has its appropriate picture in its own box. The chart is taken down and each in turn has to stand in front of the big blackboard. Teacher points to random pictures with her long cane to test us. 'aap, noot, Mies, Wim, Zus, Jet, Teun, vuur Gijs, lam, weide,' and so on.

Another chart shows the world and all its countries. There is also a map showing the whole of the Netherlands, its provinces all in different colours.

We learn where the red cattle graze or the black-and-white Friesians are, where the cherry orchards grow, where the big harbour cities are and the oil refineries spew out their smoke. We learn the names of the North Sea islands and where to find the prehistoric hut circles. I have been starved for so long of all learning material that I eagerly absorb everything I can.

During the cold winter months, the janitor lights a giant round stove in the corner of each classroom. A tall soot-covered coal bucket stands beside it. There is no fireguard, but we know the rules and keep well away from the red-hot stove.

Mid-morning the bell goes, and we are allowed our break. Before we are turned out into the playground, we all receive a quarter-litre bottle of milk. The silver tops are collected for recycling. Teacher, always concerned for our welfare, stands the crate of milk bottles right next to the stove. Cream globules float to the tops of the bottles, and the warm milk is so repugnant that each day I struggle to finish mine. But like the plateful of tomatoes sprinkled with sugar, it is 'good for you', so without complaining, I get on with it.

Deventer

Deventer is an ancient town with a weekly cattle market that is just round the corner from the 2de Pauwelandstraat where Oma and Opa live. There are shiny, worn metal bars everywhere to tie up the cattle. Very soon we learn, like every child in town, that the slippery metal bars are perfect for turning topsy-turvy. There are always children to be found round the marketplace, twisting and turning round and round and again on the bars.

On market days Opa takes a metal bucket, together with a coal scuttle, to collect his weekly steaming ration of green cow manure for his garden. Everyone living near the noisy market considers it one of the perks.

I watch for hours on end. I get close to the huge black-and-white cows that come from up north and Friesland, and the gentle brown-and-white cows that live on the river pastures further south. The rosy-cheeked farmers do their deals with the traditional handclap and spit. They are rough and ready but kind, and they sense my interest in the gentle beasts. I am often invited to duck under the bars and stroke the warm but filthy hides of the cows. No one bothers to clean the cattle before they are brought to market.

Oma goes to the fish market. Some days she will bring back a large newspaper-wrapped parcel. When opened up, it will reveal ten or more shiny, golden-brown, live eels. They are fat and wriggling in the sawdust that sticks to them. Oma goes to work chopping them up in short pieces before dropping them into the foaming butter in the huge frying pan. She tells the same story again and again. Alarmingly, she describes in detail how she will not sleep that night, as the eels inside her tummy will wriggle in protest at having been chopped up.

Beneath the house is the cellar. It runs under the whole of the house. Most Dutch houses have a cellar, as the houses are built on reclaimed land or sand, which serves as foundation for the building. It is a wonderful place, full of interesting nooks and crannies. A narrow door in the marble hall leads straight to the rickety wooden stairs. The cellar itself is divided into different areas. Brick columns support the ceiling.

Below the roadside wall is a wrought-iron grate that leads to the coal chute under the house. The coal merchant will remove the grate from the outside and tip the sacks of coal straight down the chute. If you walk along the Dutch streets you will find that each house has its own coal chute.

Also in the cellar are racks of roughly sawn timber that hold tins and glass jars filled with Oma's summer produce. There are plums, both yellow and purple, large green gherkins, white haricot beans, salted eggs, and pots of bramble jelly and jams. Large brown-glazed jars stand on the floor, filled to the brim with sliced green beans laid down in sea salt. The wooden lids are weighted down with heavy stones.

Another area is Oma's cooking place. It is close to the coal hatch, which acts as a fan. Oma comes down here to make herring fried in oil. It is called *bokking*, and it is a favourite Dutch treat, but it makes the house stink of oil for days. When she goes down into the cellar to fry her fish, Oma is quite unrecognizable. A red-chequered tea towel hides her hair, and she wears one of Opa's collarless old shirts that reach well below her knees.

The sitting room of the house is large and dark and comfortable. An enormous coal-burning stove with mica windows stands in the corner of the room. Above it, a large woollen paisley shawl is draped across the wall. In the centre of the room stands a big table, covered by a plush carpet. All Dutch houses have carpets on their tables.

There are only three comfortable chairs in the room. One is for Opa, by the window so that he can read his books as long as possible without having to turn the light on. Nearby, his side table is piled high with his books and his newspapers, neatly folded as if no one has touched them yet. His wooden box of cigars and the glass ashtray holding his empty pipe are at the back.

Oma's chair stands by the stove. Oma never simply sits in her chair. She always has something to do. It is a family trait, as my own mother always has something to do or make. She knits or sews, just like her mother before her. And I do the same. I have my tapestry, or painting, or books.

Oma sits with a basket lined with old newspaper; it is filled with potatoes to be peeled. Sometimes the basket is piled high with golden russet apples, which she peels, slices, and dips in salted water before neatly arranging them atop the wire rack above the stove. After a few days, the slices are dried and leathery, and she stores them in tall glass jars.

Oma is a knitter. Usually she makes socks on four knitting needles. I can never get enough of watching her nimble fingers and hearing the needles go *clickety-clack, clickety-clack.*

Crochet is another pastime, and Oma's home-made antimacassars are done in creamy, shiny cotton and draped across the backs of the chairs. There is another reception room, but it is cold and rarely used.

Oma and Opa died within days of each other in the early sixties, and both were laid in their coffins, on display in that cold front room for anyone coming to the house for condolences and a last look at them. That is the custom in Holland.

Above the bedrooms is another floor. It is a large loft, with proper stairs leading to it. The loft, like the cellar, is divided into different sections. There are two windows, so there is plenty of light. One third of the roof space is covered in newspapers, and apples are stored in neat rows. The smell is sweet and lovely. It is a treat to be asked to take the basket up there and fill it with apples. There are washing lines to hang the laundry to dry during the winter months.

One corner has iron rods wedged between the rafters. Coats and clothes smelling of mothballs hang in neat rows.

There are many boxes, small and large, stacked in this corner, but two shoeboxes keep me enchanted for many hours. They are packed full of butterflies—silk embroidered butterflies of every hue, in assorted sizes. There are pinks and purples, reds and blues, greens and yellows, orange and khaki. They are so beautiful, so soft, so varied, and they remind me of faraway tropics where the silk colours are vibrant.

Nicolette and I lay them out in different patterns: colour by colour, small by small, large and small mixed, or long lines reaching to the heavens, where great clouds of butterflies enchant the angels.

Many years later I am already a student nurse when Oma and Opa die, and I am roped in to clear out the house. These boxes full of 'tea coupon' butterflies are thrown away, and I am much too timid to ask if I may have them. But I remember the magic of the silk butterflies now and again for the rest of my life.

Return To Java And Bersiap (Revolution)

We have returned to the tropics, and life is changing at a fast pace. Once the Japanese left their posts, bands of politically aligned young people took their places. Dutch colonials are no longer acceptable as the ruling class, and we live in dangerous times. A revolution is being fought, and the word *merdeka* (freedom) is on everyone's lips.

Ethnic cleansing is an expression not coined yet, but a white face is a legitimate target. Even Pappie, with his dark skin and long ancestry of mixed-race family, is attacked. One day he arrives home very late, with his white tropical suit covered with black dirt. He is very shaken.

He left in the early morning to visit one of his outlying plantations by train. The freedom fighters, knowing this to be a European train, bombed the railway line. Pappie and his fellow travellers threw themselves on the floor of the carriage and escaped with their lives.

We feel this is our country too. This is where we were born, where our family has lived and worked for many generations. It is where our ancestors are buried, and yet we are despised. We are told we do not belong here. 'Go home to Froggy Land' is scrawled on the walls of our home. Our servants are loyal and carry no animosity towards us, and yet we coexist in uneasy companionship.

We have gone to live in the Opakstraat in Soerabaya, in an old colonial house with a wide veranda both front and side of the house, alongside a row of bedrooms. The rooms are large and the ceilings fifteen feet high. All the windows have mosquito grills. The rooms smell of *flitspuit*, as Baboe generously sprays the rooms twice a day to rid them of mosquitoes.

Soerabaya, an old harbour city on the north-east, swampy coast of Java, is hot. Kublai Khan's army fought a bloody battle here in 1293. It has been a commercial centre since the fourteenth century and is growing fast after the war. The melodious name is derived from the alleged battle fought between a shark, *sura*, and a crocodile, *buaya*.

As usual in the colonial houses, the servant's quarters are situated behind the main house and connected by a covered walkway. We children can be found most of the time on the blakan with the good-natured servants. They all live in the slow lane, as the climate is much too hot for doing anything in a hurry.

Each servant is allocated one household task. They enjoy the security of their jobs in these uncertain, restless times. They are genuinely fond of us despite the revolutionary propaganda machine telling them to hate us. We communicate with them in their own Malay language. We are so used to speaking Malay that Mammie frequently has to remind us to speak Dutch to her and to each other. She gets very cross when we forget. All Dutch people are expected to speak Malay; we certainly do not expect the servants to speak our language.

It is Christmas time, and for several months we have had a young turkey, bought for us by Kokkie at the market. He struts about in the back garden, tied to his post by a long piece of string safely knotted to one of his legs. Frank has discovered that if he annoys the turkey long enough, it will get angry, and its floppy wattle and comb will turn puce. Frank struts in front of the turkey, just out of reach, mimicking its *gobble, gobble, gobble* to perfection. Djongos finally intervenes and stops Frank from pestering the bird.

The day has finally arrived when the turkey will be sacrificed for our Christmas dinner. We all come out to watch the terrible deed. Baboe puts her arms around me and hides my face in her sarong, but I cannot resist peeping to watch the *kebon* (the garden boy) untie the piece of string on its leg with great care, cupping his hand round the bird's face while he slits its throat with a razor blade.

But—oh, horror of horrors—the headless bird runs away from the scene of the crime in a straight line, directly towards me! When it finally collapses in an untidy heap on the ground, its sandy legs sticking out haphazardly, it is lying right by my feet. In both horror and fascination

I can see only the bloody, gaping neck. Baboe wails and cries her dismay while squashing her brown arms round me till I can hardly breathe.

Nonchalantly Kebon collects the bloody bird and hangs it by its legs from a low branch in the cherry tree. A large enamel bowl is placed below the gaping bloody neck. It has to be bled to ensure the meat will be white. The bowl of blood is given to the servants, who will make it into sausages for themselves.

The normally quiet, peaceful evenings are full of unrest these days. We hear the young men of the city shouting their freedom chant: *merdeka! merdeka!* while we sleep our restless sleep, uncomfortably aware of the explosive danger all around us. Mammie and Pappie are talking about the situation in soft voices. Even the servants are taken under the loupe. No one can be trusted these days. The attack on the train has severely shaken the European community.

Our new school is not far away, and Nicolette and I walk all the way. I am not really a naughty child, as I am too timid to be up to too much controversy. I am nevertheless a gregarious girl and have no problem making friends. I am a chatterbox who is frequently told to be quiet. Nicolette certainly is not naughty; she is quite a withdrawn child and very serious. The discipline of our earlier childhood has seen to that. However, we do get into some scrapes, and here are two stories. Neither has left me with any real sense of guilt, while the turmoil it created at the time leaves no doubt in my mind as to the severity of the deeds!

On our way to school we pass the KNIL (*Koninklijk Nederlands Indische Landmacht* or the Dutch East Indies Army) barracks. The camp has the same bamboo matting round its perimeter as we had round the POW camp. Only this time we are on the outside. It is quite easy to peep inside, as there are plenty of very small gaps in the matting for a little girl to squash her eye against.

I am insatiably curious and often drive my elders frantic with my constant stream of questions. I am also a perfect target for teasing by my peers, as I am only too willing to please and do as I am told. Today the small group of friends tell me to go, have a look, and tell them what I can see. Right in front of my eyes I see a long line of open-air showers, in constant use by the soldiers. I am so completely absorbed by what I am seeing that it escapes my attention that my friends have scampered off. Then I feel myself being grabbed by the scruff of my neck.

A young officer pulls me away from the fence and marches me off to the commanding officer, a big burly man with a shock of ginger hair and a neat ginger moustache. He is clearly at loss as to what to do with this small girl. In the end, I am lifted into a jeep and sat beside the officer, thoroughly enjoying the ride. I am not taken to school but home to face the music.

In the 1940s in the Far East, nakedness is nothing to be ashamed of. Most locals bathe in the brown waters of the rivers. The beautiful girls go mostly topless, and ablutions are performed without much discretion.

My parents give me a severe reprimand, but I am aware of an undercurrent of great amusement. It is quite a dilemma for the adults how to handle this small girl with an issue that really is not an issue. I am, however, never allowed to forget about it, and the story is repeated among my parents' friends at every opportunity!

The second story concerns learning about right and wrong. Nicolette and I have 'found' a ten-guilder note lying on Mammie's dressing table. The dressing table holds a host of fascinating items. There is a large, round pot of cold cream, along with brushes, a tortoiseshell comb and mirror, and small bottles of scent. Occasionally we are allowed a tiny spot of Mille Fleurs scent on the inside of a wrist.

The bank note is available for the taking. Somewhere in the recesses of our children's minds there is the realization that this money in not legitimately found, but we take it nevertheless and plot and plan what to do with it.

There is a small toko (shop) on our way to school that sells, among other things, sweets of every colour and taste. During our camp years we never knew the taste of sweets, and in post-war Indies sweets are still a rarity for most children. Sweets are only on offer at birthday parties or when we are invited to the Dutch Embassy to celebrate the queen's birthday.

To spend a ten-guilder note—the equivalent of many months' wages for any of the servants—on sweets is going to need some planning. Nicolette is in charge, and she leads us into the toko, where we make our purchase. My favourite sweet is the *lombok* sweet. It is red and shaped like a fiery red pepper. If you suck it slowly, the point becomes razor-sharp, and it lasts forever. Then there are assem sweets, made from the tamarind pods and covered in sugar. There is *ting djai*, a spicy biscuit; *katjang goreng* (fried peanuts); *aroe manis*, made from sugar cane; and many more to choose from. Without blinking an eye, we set to spend what must seem a small fortune to the shopkeeper.

He does not complain, and he produces a very large cardboard box for us to carry the hoard. At home we hide the large box in the bottom of our wardrobe. Soon enough Mammie discovers the disappearance of her ten-guilder note.

Each of the servants is sternly questioned. They all throw up their hands, protesting their innocence. After serious discussion, my parents decide to call in the police. The chief inspector is a family friend, and he arrives at the house in his smart, crisp uniform, carrying the voice of authority. Once again the servants are interviewed, one by one.

Kokkie is dramatically wailing her innocence, begging to be believed. She does not want to lose her job. She would never think of stealing, and she never comes into bedrooms, anyway.

Baboe Dalem is the only one who deals with bedrooms. Like Kokkie, she wails and weeps and squats on the floor, burying her head in her lap. And still we do not own up—as by now the whole matter has got very much out of hand.

In the end, Djongos is dismissed, as he is young and suspected of being a merdeka fighter anyway. Some days later, our half-empty box is discovered, and that is when we finally own up. The remaining sweets are taken away, and we are made to apologize to Kokkie, Baboe, and the rest of the servants. Bread and water is our punishment for three days.

It surely has been a very serious offence to take such a large amount of money and allow the servants to be suspected of stealing. It should have set my alarm bells ringing, but alas, I regret to say that to me it never did seem the big crime it was, just a waste of a great many nice sweets.

Such is the innocence of childhood!

ST.Theresa Prayer

May today there be peace within,
May you trust that you are exactly where you
are meant to be.
May you not forget the infinite possibilities
that are born of faith in yourself and others.
May you use the gifts that you have received
and pas on the love that has been given to you,
May you be content with yourself just the way you are,
Let this knowledge settle into your bones, and allow your soul
the freedom to sing, dance, praise and love.
It is there for each and every one of us.

Watching The World Go By

Nicolette and I belong to a small singing group, and once every two weeks we are picked up by a large, black, shiny car, chauffeur driven, to go to the other side of Soerabaya, where there is a small recording studio. Our singing is recorded for the local radio programme.

I am a very sanguine, good-natured child, without moods or sulks. My baby book records that I never remain angry for very long and never hold a grudge. I am known by friends and family as *zonnestraaltje*, which is the Dutch word for little sunbeam. However the recording sessions make me very nervous.

No one shouts or puts undue pressure on us, and we enjoy learning many new songs. Singing is a Dutch pastime and an important part of our education. Every child learns to sing; Mammie sings, and Nicolette and I soon learn to sing in harmony. The whole family sings. So why are the recording sessions making me so nervous?

The answer most likely lies in the legacy of camp years that have left me without much self-confidence, oversensitive to any kind of criticism, and with an ingrained expectation to be humiliated and put down. I am conditioned to feel unworthy and will spend most of my life struggling to come to terms with the knowledge that in truth I am a child of God and therefore worthy. The easy answer to stop my nerves from overtaking me is to take me away from the singing group. So Nicolette continues to sing, and I remain home.

I love watching our wide street and all the life it contains. There are huge kanari trees lining each side of the road. When the kanari nuts, with their fleshy texture, are ripe we collect the fallen ones and spend the afternoon on the veranda cracking the nuts between two stones.

The *toekang ramboet* (barber) has set up shop in the cool shadow of the trees. He has a nail in the tree to hang his mirror; his wooden box containing comb, scissors, soap, and a bottle of coconut hair oil; and a white sheet to drape round his customers. A three-legged stool, and a broom to sweep together the pile of black hair, and the toekang ramboet is content to sit and await a steady stream of men and boys in need of haircuts.

There is much laughter and kretek-smoking among the group of onlookers. All the men sit on their haunches, watching the world go by. Feet wide apart, buttocks gently resting on the lower part of the legs, and arms dangling across the knees, they squat. Sixty years later, I am still able to djonkok for hours on end!

Not far away, two women sit delousing each other. I am happy to watch this social intercourse. The squashing of a louse between the two thumbnails gives a satisfying little pop. The two women are doing each other a favour.

In our Western culture, to carry each other's burden rarely amounts to more than the expression of a polite 'How are you?' Other people's problems are not often taken on board unconditionally, and we are all afraid of letting others invade our precious privacy. But in this culture-rich land, social intercourse is structured on small, peaceful chores performed in daily exchange between friends and family. Neighbourly bonding is an important part of life. It results in a generosity of spirit rarely witnessed in Western cultures.

Many years later, I return to my homeland on a British passport, remembering the revolution and the removal of our family and all their possessions from the island of Java. I pretend I am British, not Dutch, in the hope that they will not find out I am the daughter of a former colonial. But how wrong and Western it is to think that way!

When these lovely people realize my past, they are excited and hail me as one of their own. Oh, you are an *orang Soerabaya* (a person born in, and therefore belonging to, Soerabaya). So I am hugged and called 'one of us'. The past is forgiven—but not just that. The past is part of today and tomorrow.

Learning About A New World

Today is Queen Wilhelmina's birthday. There is an invitation for the whole family to come and celebrate the day at the Dutch embassy. For the children there is an extra-special treat, as we are going to see our very first film. I have not an inkling what watching a film means, but I hear that the story is about Gulliver and his travels.

We have to look smart, and our clothes are washed, starched, and ironed by Tjoetie. Mammie is a wonderful dressmaker and makes all our clothes, together with the Javanese *djait* (seamstress).

All Javanese do their work squatting down on the floor. Kokkie cooks our meals djongkokking around her battery of charcoal and paraffin burners. Djait sits at a table just thirty centimetres off the floor. She makes Mammie's dresses, while Mammie sews for the four children.

All Mammie's cocktail dresses are made from shiny silks. There are beautiful wide, long skirts topped with matching tulle overskirts. Some dresses are so narrow at the hem that Mammie can only walk in them if she takes tiny little steps on her high-heeled shoes. Some silks are embossed with embroidered flowers, while others are boldly striped yellow and black.

My dresses are cotton, and today I will be wearing my favourite white dress. It has a wide skirt that obligingly balloons when I twirl. Mammie has embroidered a wide band of colourful flowers around the hem. A long bow at the back finishes it off.

When we tumble out of the big black Buick, the Embassy staff are waiting for us behind long white-clothed tables piled high with tiny sandwiches, crunchy biscuits, sweetmeats wrapped in banana leaves, truffles rolled in coconut, and orangeade.

An enormous photograph of the queen hangs in a prominent position, orange silk ribbons draped round it. Red-white-and-blue flags hang from the numerous white poles.

The brass band strikes up with the Dutch national anthem. Any child not standing to attention is quickly hauled up on his or her feet, as it is a sign of disrespect to do otherwise.

The adults get together over drinks, while the children play games on the sweeping wide lawns bordered by large flower beds. When most of the goodies are gone, the children are brought into a darkened room. The staff explain that in order to see the film we have to sit in the dark, but there is nothing to be afraid of.

I'm sure it is hard for the modern child to imagine what life without film or TV would be like. For us it is a new world coming to light, and as the story of little people, a giant traveller, strange landscapes and costumes unfolds, our fantasies take a giant leap into a new world.

A Child In A Foster Home

We have returned to Holland, this time by aeroplane. It is a forty-eight-hour journey, and the plane has made two overnight stops, one in Baghdad and one in Cairo. There are many other stops in between.

In Cairo I fall rather badly while trying to skip along the gravelled path going to our hotel. A lot of gravel gets wedged in my grazed knees. A *bourdous*-wearing Arab sweeps me up and bundles me in his voluminous robes, assuring Mammie that it is all right; he will bring me back once he has dealt with the wounds. The airport first-aid people are very nice, and they fuss over me, offering me sweet dates while they clean me up and apply a wonderful bandage to my leg. It has been worth all the pain and shock.

It is winter, and we can only fly as far as Paris airport in France, due to heavy snow and ice at Schiphol airport. So we finish the trip by train, which is just as exciting. We will be staying with Oma and Opa in Deventer.

Life in Holland is slowly returning to some kind of normality. This war-torn country is getting itself back on its feet, but rationing still dominates daily life. Oma manages to cook nutritional meals and always more than enough for our large family. However, a dark shadow hangs over my life. Mammie has placed an advert in the national papers: 'Good home sought for two little girls.'

There is no boarding-school system in Holland; it is considered preferable to leave planters' children behind in Holland with foster families so that they may benefit from the superior education system.

Thousands of children are left behind each year, placed with complete strangers. It is part of the system, and children do not question it, nor do parents consider it wrong. There is one consolation: Nicolette and I will be together.

There are plenty of people willing to adopt children from a different environment for a few years, as the financial rewards are considerable. Four years after the war, cash is in short supply. Mammie sorts the possible suitable homes from the not so suitable, and eventually a few are chosen for inspection. Mammie, Nicolette, and I board the train.

This is, of course, a two-way inspection. Either party may think the arrangement not to their taste. Nicolette and I may well be rejected. It is a strange experience to go family-hunting! I am very much aware of being only a tiny cog in the decision-making machine. Indeed, the final decision will be made for me.

For a number of days we traipse from one address to another. We look over some homes in The Hague, and a lovely family with two girls of our own age group seems a possibility. The home is bright and cheerful, filled with well-cared-for potted plants, books, and pale birch-wood furniture. I am intrigued by large purple curtains sparkling with moons and stars. It all seems perfect, and we chat about every detail excitedly on the journey home. We are quite certain they will accept us. Two days later, when they phone to say they have changed their minds, the feeling of rejection is overwhelming. The pain is so great that I sob my heart out, but I am called a crybaby.

Two days later a family is found just half an hour's walk from where Oma and Opa live. This is close enough for us to make plenty of visits. We are to call these people Tante and Oom.

Their small house is in a long street. It smells musty inside, and we soon realize that this household revolves around the 14-year-old son. He is very clever, studious, and so-o-o-o boring. The entire family is overweight. They are, however, not unkind, but the invasion of two small girls from the faraway colonies is not quite what they are prepared for.

We say a tearful goodbye to our family, who will be leaving to return to Soerabaya. Little do we know that we shall not meet again till four years later.

I am 8 years old.

It is soon clear that the family have no idea how to care for two small girls. For my once-a-month hair wash I am sent to the hairdresser's. There is no bathroom, and we are washed in the kitchen sink. The clothes Tante buys for us are many sizes too large, and we look like scarecrows. Everything is bought for growth, and Oma tries to intervene. Tante complains that we spend far too much time with family and she thinks their influence may be detrimental. After a whole year of tension, the decision is made for us to find another family.

Mammie's sister, Lena, finds us a placing with the local Dutch Reformed minister. The house is a big three-story one, and our bedroom is right at the top of the second flight of stairs. Only a bare dim bulb lights the staircase, and I am always afraid to go up by myself. The lime-green paint that covers all the walls is flaking, and there is a general sense of poverty about the place. Our bedroom is spartan. There are no curtains or pictures on the walls, no heating, and it is bitterly cold during the long Dutch winters. There is nothing homely about this place.

There are five children in this family, and Nicolette and I fit in somewhere in the middle. This 'tante' is always crabby, overworked, irritated, and very unkind to us. There is a lot of shouting in this family. All the children gang up against us and constantly tell tales to get us into trouble. This is a family that will spend their life making us miserable and finding ways of getting me to cry. Nicolette is so much more stoic than I am; I can see her clamping her mouth shut rather than crying.

Tante is obsessive about our language. It seems that whatever we say she finds fault with, and she knows a perfect cure for little girls who do not speak correctly. Almost weekly she roughly grabs me and mashes soft green soap into my mouth, rubbing it round and round my gums till the froth almost chokes me. 'Now, Hanneke, rinse, and rinse, and rinse again till your mouth is cleansed from all that sin!'

Mealtimes are agony, as Tante is also obsessive about table manners. She torments me relentlessly about my manners. 'Don't hang in your chair, Hanneke—sit up straight!' Soon enough the dreaded broom comes out of the cupboard, and I am tied tightly to the broom against the back of the chair. For the rest of the meal I endure the sniggers and humiliation from the rest of the family. But I will learn to eat my meals sitting up straight.

Most of our meals consist of bread with a smudge of margarine. We are only allowed one slice of bread with a slice of cheese or a scraping of jam on it. The rest is known as 'bread with contentment'. More often than not the cheese is taken away before I have a chance to ask for a slice. Tante loves to taunt. She holds the cheese aloft, moving it from left to right. 'Cheese, cheese, anyone for cheese?' she says with a smile, looking me straight in the eye. But before I have a chance to nod my head, she loudly announces, 'If no one wants the cheese, the cheese goes back in the cupboard.' And indeed it does. If I dare protest, she sneers at me and tells me I should have been quicker off the mark.

I have become a 'crybaby', and I am locked up in the bathroom for so long that surely there cannot be a tear left inside me. Still hiccupping with deep sorrow for myself, I am finally released from my prison many hours later.

To the Dutch, birthdays are important. In this family it is traditional to be allowed to choose the menu. In the post-war days of shortages and few treats, this is an important occasion for everyone—a special meal.

January 6, Epiphany or The Kings' Day, as it is known in Holland, is the birthday of one of the girls. She has chosen a king's meal indeed. There will be roast beef, French fries, peas, and apple sauce, with a chocolate blancmange for pudding. The table is set, her chair decorated with paper flowers, and we are all excited for the evening's event. Tante calls Nicolette and me and tells us to put our coats on. She instructs us to go to the gym club we belong to, as tonight there is a special event. We are puzzled, as neither of us remember any festivities other than the birthday.

'What about the birthday meal?' we ask.

'Never mind that; you shall eat when you return. You must go *now*!'

It is bitterly cold, and there is snow on the ground.

Nicolette and I walk the hour-long journey into town holding hands. The gym club lies in a narrow, dark street; there is almost no street lighting. Most of the warehouses are derelict or abandoned, and I am very afraid. There is peeling paint on the closed door, and we quickly start the long walk back home, away from this desolate place. But the table is empty, the food gone, and a slice of bread our only evening meal.

Winters in Holland are very cold, and the houses have no heating. For the past year I have become a bundle of nerves and have started to wet my bed.

The cruelty of this family, their constant humiliations, and the bitterly cold nights have had a profound effect on me. I lie shaking for hours between the sheets before exhaustion sends me into an uneasy sleep.

I make my own bed in the mornings, and I think I can hide the big yellow tell-tale patches on the white sheets if I make my bed neatly enough. But Tante screams her displeasure, and she taunts me about being a rich planter's child with disgusting habits and being a crybaby. Her ultimate threat is that she will no longer wash my sheets, and I will have to lie on those sheets for the rest of my life. There is an overwhelming sense of failure and guilt constantly with me.

One bitterly cold day I find my sheets have been replaced with full-size rubber ones. All night I lie desperately searching for a little warmth between the rubber sheets. I wake every morning lying in a pool of frozen urine. But there is always Nicolette. She cleans the mess, she hugs me, she plaits my hair, she pulls my dress straight, she consoles me, and she loves me.

Summer arrives, and we talk about holidays. We are going to go camping. It sounds a wonderful adventure. There will be tents and meals by a fire. There will be walks and treats, and we are all part of one big family.

Our grey cardboard suitcase is packed, and we are ready to go. Only no one has bothered to tell us that we are not going to be included. A large black taxi has come to collect us, and it is only then that we realize we shall not be part of this camping trip at all. Nicolette and I are taken to a pension out in the country, where we shall spend the better part of our summer holidays. There are no other children. There's nothing to do, but we have been told to behave and do what we are told. We will be collected in a few weeks' time. The elderly couple running the pension will keep an eye on us. I am not yet 10 years old.

Sunday is church day, and Dominee (the minister) conducts his services. There is never a mention of Jesus in this family, and there is no evidence that this family love Him or know about Him. We see very little of this henpecked man. Most days he tucks himself away in his study, escaping the noise of seven children and the wrath of his angry, overworked wife. But today he is expecting his brother and his wife.

Nicolette and I feel outsiders when they visit. It is not surprising. When his brother arrives, the children are summoned for a treat. We are told to hold out our hands, and he drops a twenty-five-cent coin into each one, but when it is our turn we are told, 'Not for you—you are not family.' Each day is one of rejection.

There is no love in this family, just cruelty and denial.

Another New Family

The new family we are going to live with consists of Tante, Uncle, and their very small daughter. There is also a dog, called Tjong. He is a chow chow, who needs a good brushing every day and has a purple tongue. At the bottom of the garden is a long run with five hens and a cockerel. I am in seventh heaven!

Before long I have picked up lots of interesting facts about this family. Tante is boss in the home. What she demands happens. She will stand for no nonsense. Don't cross Tante, or your life is not worth living. She suffers from 'nerves' and spends the afternoon hours in bed; she is often tired, although the household is not very big and Uncle does a lot of the chores.

Tante has had a number of miscarriages in her life, and I spend many hours looking at the small photograph of their baby, Jacob, who only lived a few hours. The photograph was taken when Jacob was already dead, and I cannot keep my eyes from his tiny, sweet face. The little girl has been adopted, and the family speak about it quite openly.

Tante has been a nurse, and everything in the home is run like a well-organized hospital. Sheets on the beds are made with hospital corners, and every week the bottom sheet is removed to be replaced by the top sheet. A fresh top sheet is put on every Monday. Inspections are carried out every week to ensure Nicolette and I make our beds exactly according to the rules.

Tante is in control of everything in our lives, Uncle's life, the little daughter's life, Tjong's life, and even the lives of the run full of chickens. If things do not go according to her wishes, which is very often, Tante starts to scream and cry and throw with her glasses. It is very tiring and disconcerting.

I have made some lovely new friends, however, just a few doors down. It is a large, relaxed family in which they all tease each other good-naturedly. Their home is chaotic and friendly. The children have a table full of special children's magazines, which they readily lend us. These are mostly Donald Duck and other cartoon characters. But Tante takes one look at the sinful magazines and insists we take them back and never look at them again. They are full of corruption and evil and will destroy us for sure.

Some weeks later I manage to sneak in another of the magazines, but Tante almost has a heart attack when she discovers it. I am told that if ever I bring one into the house again, she will send me away for good.

The truth is that Tante is not coping very well with two extra children in the house. Both Nicolette and I are quite timid; we are painfully polite, anxious to do the right thing, and acutely aware of being the cause of so much disruption. My nerves are dangling by a thread.

The chicken run becomes my escape route if things get too hard to bear. But I have not lost my sense of fun; I collect silly jokes, which I repeat all day long, till everyone tells me to shut up! Nicolette and I have both learned to be stoic in the face of trauma, but the two of us suffer from a lack of self-confidence. We are also growing up fast.

It has been seven years since we last lived with our own family, and we do not seem to belong to anyone. In those days it was normal for the children of colonial families to be sent to Holland for their education.

But there is no boarding school system in Holland so most children were placed in foster families.

Travel in those days was very expensive and slow. A flight to Holland would take 48 hours with an overnight stop staying in a Hotel somewhere in the Middle East in Baghdad, Damascus, Haifa or Cairo. Companies would not pay for what were then very expensive flights to the other side of the world,

Our parents took European leave every 3 or 4 years. So we often would not see each other for 3 or 4 years. We only communicated by letter and those would take 7 or 10 days to arrive.

This is a very unhappy time, and it comes as a great relief when we are told we are to return to our homeland for eight weeks during the summer holidays. It will give everyone a break from times fraught with anxiety.

The Turmoil Of Politics

I am 15 years old, and I am basking in the pleasure of being back home. on the island of Java. I soak up the familiar atmosphere, the gentle pace, the comfort of the language, the luxury of servants, the abundant landscape, the vibrant colours of the tropics, but most of all, being together as a family.

Soon after we return to Europe, we are once again moved to another family. Tante has realized during our long absence that she really does not want to cope with us any longer. Our parents have realized that this highly charged, nervous household is not doing us much good. We move to Bussem, not far from Hilversum, so that we do not have to change schools again. We will have moved school eleven times by the time we are old enough to leave. Our brother, Frank, also lives in Bussem, where he lodges with another family.

For the first time, our new family turns out to be just perfect. This next Tante is a widow who lost her husband in a Japanese concentration camp. As a child she, too, was sent to foster families in Holland. She has two much older teenage children herself.

She understands us better than anyone has done before. She will stand for no nonsense and expects us to pull our weight, but she loves us, and the house rings with lots of laughter. She understands our lack of confidence and encourages us continually. For the first time in my life I know that here is someone who will protect me and love me just as I am.

It is the year 1957, and anyone carrying a Dutch passport in the former colonies is ordered to leave the country. Within weeks, whole families are uprooted from their homes. Thousands of Dutch-passport-carrying individuals who have never before set foot on Dutch soil and who have considered the Far East their home, are being transported by the planeload back to 'froggy land'. Thus, for the second time, my family arrives in Holland under refugee status. We come with hardly any belongings to our name.

Holland is being invaded by thousands of migrants of every hue and colour, most without homes or jobs.

Mammie buys a newly built house in the village of Hollandsche Rading, where we are going to have to learn to live together as a family.

Pappie, however, is too young to retire; he has a large family to support. As a planter, he will never find a job in the already-overcrowded job market in Holland. He finds a job in Ghana, West Africa, where I join him a year later for some months before becoming an au pair girl in Yorkshire, England.

Being An Aux-Pair In England, 1958– 59

I have spent the night in The Hague with Pappie's aunt, Tante Pleun. She is another member of our family who has been forcibly removed from the Far East to live in Holland.

The house, as always, is full of smiling, generous aunts, uncles, nieces, and nephews, working together in the kitchen, preparing food. Food is an important part of the family. It is not Dutch food but proper Indonesian food. It consists of rice with many other dishes. The familiar wonderful smells put everyone in a happy mood. Tante Pleun is a dear. She is old and fat, and her sparse grey hair is bundled in a tiny knot at the back of her head. She has realized my extreme shyness among so many people, but no matter. She puts me to work in the kitchen, where I soon get caught up in the laughter and preparations. The house is full to bursting, but everyone is welcome to share. It is so comfortable to hear the heavily accented voices.

All colonials speak Dutch with rolling r's, their own colloquial language, liberally sprinkled with *'Adoe sheh ja'* (this is almost non translatable, but something like" goodness gracious me, or"heavens above ")).

There is none of the Dutch aloofness and rigidity in this bunch of Dutch people. It is almost as if they are a different nation. And of course, so they are. Born and brought up in the hot, colourful, Spice Islands below the equator, these people have brought their easy-going lifestyle with them to their cold and crowded motherland.

My nephew Ido kindly takes me to the docks in Hoek van Holland (Hook of Holland) the following day, where I am to catch the ferry to Harwich. It will bring a new phase in my life, and although I am quite nervous, I am excited, too. I shall be spending the best part of a year with a family in England to improve my English. Becoming an au pair is the *in* thing to do. Many of my school friends do this before embarking on a career or taking a university place. Languages are very important to the Dutch, as many college textbooks are written in English, French, or German.

On the ferry, I team up with a kindly soul who is off to see her daughter, married to an Englishman and about to have a new baby. Together we catch the train to the north, and on the station there is no shortage of willing staff to carry my luggage and take me to the right platform. My destination is Yorkshire and Harrogate.

Peggy Trier, my employer for the next nine months, is waiting on the platform. Against her ample bosom and tucked from within her woollen jumper peeps a most beautiful brown-eyed, black-haired baby girl. Many years later, Peggy confessed that she took one look at me and thought with despair, *My God, this girl is shy!* And of course, so I was—painfully shy, even without the language barrier.

My suitcase is dumped into the back of the car, next to the baby carrier, and not long afterwards I get my first glimpse of the ancient cathedral town of Ripon.

A short drive through the countryside, and we arrive at a huge pair of handsome wrought-iron gates, cross a cattle grid, and drive into a park. I have arrived at my new home, and it is not a bit like anything I have expected. The many acres of parkland will be my garden, and I can see a herd of deer looking at us from a distant hill.

This is Studley Royal, the grounds of the twelfth-century Cistercian Fountains Abbey, on the edge of Pateley Moors. It's close to the place where Wensleydale cheeses are made.

'The Cottage', which will be my home, is not a bit like a cottage in the true sense of the word. There are six bedrooms and kitchens, scullery, and pantry of enormous scale. The drawing room—with huge, comfortable, chintz-covered sofas and chairs and the luxurious skin of a polar bear on the floor—is much too big to be heated, except for use on special occasions. The house is always cold, and the only heating available is by coal and log fires and a cream-coloured solid-fuel AGA in the kitchen.

Above the AGA hangs a pulley drying rack, which is always overloaded with brown and grey school uniforms. Outside is a large concrete yard with outbuildings, full of ancient cars for Robert Trier to tinker with.

The 'garden' is surrounded by a six-foot chain-link fence to keep the deer out. It is not really a garden, just a rough patch of grass with long washing lines stretched across, propped up by hefty wooden poles.

From the kitchen I can see the little Gothic Church of Saint Mary where the Marquess of Ripon is entombed.

Peggy Trier (Mrs Trier to me) is unlike anyone else I know. She will have an enormous influence on my life, and very soon she will be able to draw out all the positive, fun elements of my personality. She is short, rotund, raven haired, rather beautiful, a chain smoker, and a down-to-earth, no-nonsense woman.

She is also the mother of five lively children. The eldest, John, is only a few years younger than I am. Charley will be born after I leave. Diana, Gillian, Jane, and baby Catharine come next, in that order. I have not learned to say the *th* sound in English, and Cathy becomes Cassy to me. Alas, she will be stuck with that name for the rest of her life.

Life with the Triers will become one of my happiest memories. They take me as they see me. They never know of my reputation at home, the nervous, insecure teenager, or any details about my earlier life.

With such a big family there is always work to be done, and I am not shy of hard work. I learn to bake cakes, two every week, and one of them is always a Parkin cake—rich and brown and gone in no time! Peggy teaches me to mix butter with margarine for post war cheapness (!) to line the piles of sandwiches for tea time. I learn about the delights of huge Sunday-roast lunches with tipsy pudding for afters.

Cooked breakfasts are the order of the day, a major undertaking for such a large family. The children are all very different, and I enjoy them all. My English comes on in leaps and bounds, and within six weeks I am more or less fluent.

John and I strike up a friendship, and we go off in the park together, to spy on the baby deer that are often hidden in the dense thistle patches. John shows me the ruins of the abbey and the steep-sided valley of the park, the water gardens, canals, and pools all fed by the little River Skell.

In March I am overwhelmed when I find there are millions of snowdrops lining the grassy slopes by the canals. I have never seen anything quite like it; it is my introduction to England's many untamed places where wild flowers can be found in great profusion.

In autumn we go off before breakfast to collect great big baskets full of flat mushrooms.

In the long summer evenings I take my sketching pad and spend many happy hours recording the ruins of the abbey. I always have the place to myself, with only the herd of deer for company and the occasional glimpse of Nelly, the fat, semi-wild pony that belongs to the Trier family. No one seems to ride the pony, and they only catch her occasionally, to have her feet trimmed under protest. The park is privately owned, with the owners living at the nearby Fountains Hall.

Another thing John and I do is set up a darkroom under the stairs, where we develop and print the pictures I take with my little Brownie camera.

At Easter we pack to the hilt the two family cars, one towing the caravan, and set off for the Lake District. It is my first introduction to camping and roaming the English countryside. It is also an introduction to historic castles, archaeology, and local history. The wild flowers so very different from the Dutch ones and so much more profuse.

I learn about fish and chips wrapped in newspaper at £4 for eight portions.

I may be in this household to take care of the children, but Peggy takes her responsibility of teaching me to speak correct English very seriously. A Dutch accent won't do, and she has me repeat a word over and over all day long until it comes out correctly.

I am also given my very first driving lessons in the park. Peggy generously tells me to take the old station wagon out in the park on my own, but on the whole I am much too timid to do so.

In the summer months, when all the children are home, we pack up the cars and the caravan once again and set off for Northumberland, to explore beaches and visit the Farne Islands in a tiny open boat. We cross the tidal road to reach Holy Island and visit numerous castles. Then it's northwards to Scotland and more exciting places to visit.

In the sheltered bays we find the small oysters that, when prised open, reveal tiny black pearls that delight me so much.

Back home in Yorkshire, on Sunday mornings we worship in the ancient cathedral of Ripon. It is my first encounter with the Anglican Church, with its pomp and ceremony, so completely missing in the Dutch

Reformed Churches. I quite fall in love with the ancient language used in the services.

All too soon my time at Studley Royal comes to an end. I have put on weight, learned to be fluent in English, had my eyes opened to the beauty of the English countryside, taught my lovely children some funny Dutch words and songs, shed some of my extreme shyness, and gained a little in confidence. Reluctantly I bid farewell to this lovely place, say goodbye to this lovely family, and return home to start my career in nursing.

My Nursing Years, 1959–1963

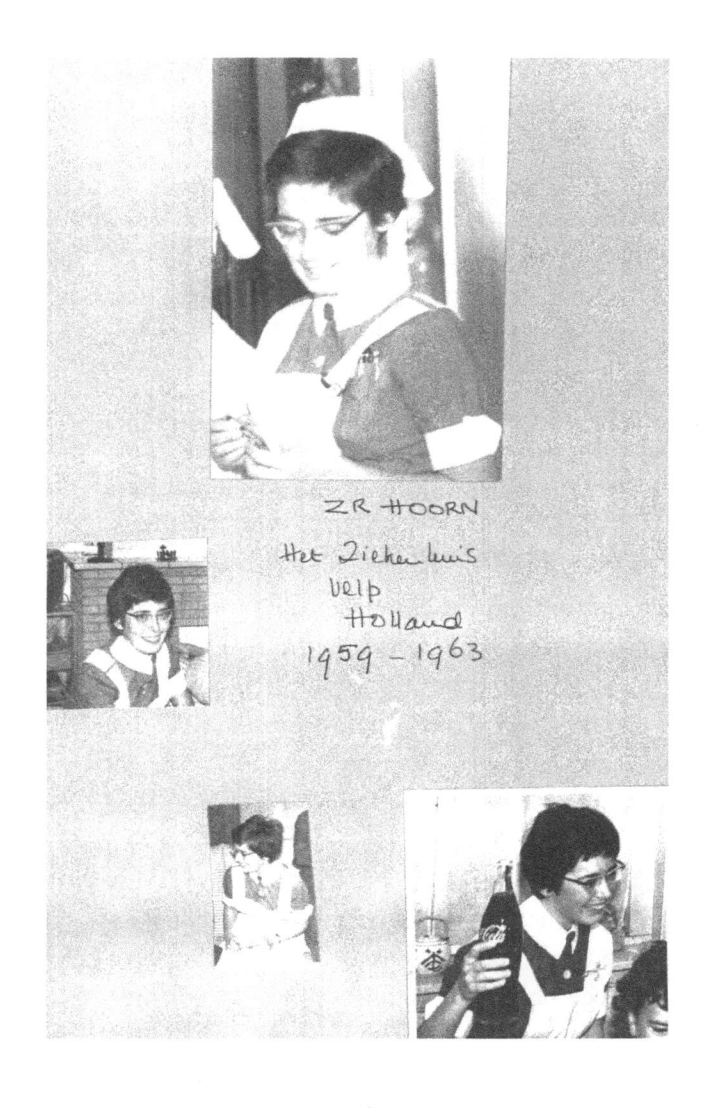

ZR HOORN
Het Ziekenhuis
Velp
Holland
1959 – 1963

Vereniging Het Ziekenhuis is a small hospital founded in 1892 in Velp, Gelderland. The hospital lies in a quiet street just off the main road running through this town in the east of Holland. The hospital is well known nationally for its excellent training, despite its small size. When I joined it a little more than sixty years later, there were about 175 beds and 70 personnel. Our laboratory measured nine by nine metres! One big theatre served the three or four surgeons connected with the hospital. Nurses were housed in several old houses within minutes' walk from the hospital. First-year students lived in the attics of the main hospital, sharing bedrooms with one or two others. There were only two showers for all of us, and most were steamy and wet when I used them; they were rarely left empty long enough to dry out. Young girls were expected to be 'in house' no later than 10.30 at night, having clocked in with the porter.

Anyone turning up later would be called to Matron's office the following day for a dressing down. Our social life was carefully scrutinized by senior staff. Everyone always knew what we were up to. If we failed in any way at all, a dressing down by Matron could be expected.

I remember on one occasion being called into Matron's office and being given a lecture on the shortness of my new haircut. I was told I was a girl, not a boy, and it did not become a nurse of that hospital to turn up with my hair cut too short!

In second year, a nurse would be given a shared room in one of the large Victorian houses near the hospital. My salary was about f10 per month (about the equivalent then of £5), well below the average. We were told that our training was exceptional, and so we could take it or leave it. There were plenty more keen prospective nurses in the waiting. It simply did not occur to me, or any of us, to question our pay packet. We were grateful for the training. All meals were provided, and all laundry was free. My pay packet was pocket money, not a salary. It was enough to pay for a train ticket home, small gifts for friends and family, and the occasional new item of clothing.

We had to purchase our uniforms. I started life as a nurse owning three blue dresses, six aprons, four caps, and three sets of cuffs. I was only allowed to wear black stockings and soft-soled black shoes. (Wearing beige stockings became a privilege only after qualification.) My cufflinks were made of bone. No jewellery of any kind was allowed, and hair could be short (but feminine!) or long but had to be scraped away from the face and tied up.

I changed my dress every other day and my apron once a day. Caps and cuffs were so stiffly starched that they remained 'clean' for a long time and were changed once a week only, unless soiled by working on a particularly bloody patient. There were over-gowns, for various dirty jobs, hanging on the backs of doors. Each nurse was allowed her own individual way of folding her cap. Our laundry, including our mufti, would be returned to our rooms within twenty-four hours.

We worked nine hours a day, with a short break for coffee, tea, and lunch, six days a week. There were just three kinds of duty: early, late, or night. Officially a forty-five-hour, five-day week came into being in 1961, but most of us continued to work well in excess of that for some time to come. In cases of emergency (which happened quite frequently, as we dealt with most accidents as well as day-to-day cases for many miles around) every nurse would be expected to pull her weight, without extra payment. Two free days could only be 'collected' at the end or beginning of each fortnight. We were allowed two weeks' holiday per year. A list with the names of all nurses in order of seniority, together with a calendar, would appear in the dining room at the start of each year. A two-week holiday could only be decided on when your name came up. The more junior, the more awful the time of the year when you got your holiday, as only one or two nurses at a time could be spared. My holiday could only be taken during the month of November for my first two years.

Night duty came at two-week stints, with an extra day off at each end.

My first encounter with Matron, or Zr (Sister) Fokker, is when I am being interviewed. The nursing staff is generally recruited from girls from the middle classes after a short interview with Matron. Zr Fokker appears to be kind but with a no-nonsense attitude. Her grey uniform with its starched collar, cuffs, and cap crackles. She is the only nurse in the entire hospital allowed long sleeves and the wearing of a sombre navy cardigan. And, of course, she does not wear an apron. She certainly inspires respect on account of her upright appearance alone.

Zr Fokker's method of interview is typically stern and serious and slightly intimidating. She is not interested in school achievements but will decide whether I am to become part of her staff on her personal assessment of me alone! Her first question is, 'Why do you want to become a nurse?'

When I tell her that my ideal is to go and work in deepest and darkest Africa and to join Dr Albert Schweitzer at his clinic in Lambarene, she takes a long, hard, silent look at me and then warns me that Dr Schweitzer is a very difficult man to work for. 'You do your training here first, and I expect you may well change your mind. Nursing is very hard work, and only a few survive the rigours of training.'

But such is the idealistic thinking of youth that I remember silently snorting and thinking, *She does not know what tough stuff I am made of.*

I am to join the new batch of trainees in June. During the first three months of training we are known as 'white mice' on account of the white, badly fitting, coats we wear. Officially my three-year training on the wards does not begin until the first three months have passed.

After a long day of nursing theory, learning the finer points of bed-making, hygiene, surgery, how to shave a patient (even in those awkward places!), how to lift, and so on, we are introduced to different departments each day, to familiarize ourselves with the entire hubbub of the hospital. Our very first task is to be allowed to take the temperature and pulse of patients. My first ward is a medical male ward. The men all know that I am a new recruit and have prepared a little joke for me. Temperatures are taken by rectum. There are sixteen beds on the ward. As I turn each sheet to insert the thermometer, a flower greets me, sticking out from the buttocks. Each new patient winks at me wickedly and silently mouths, 'For you.' To say I am embarrassed is an understatement, but the story serves to be told and creates plenty of merriment, for many years to come.

Generally speaking, the men on the ward are very protective of the young girls and always put in a good word when the ward sister publicly tears strips off us when jobs have not been done to perfection.

To be publicly told off and humiliated is all part of the discipline and certainly teaches us to know our place in the hierarchy of the hospital. We get to know every part of the hospital intimately, from the kitchens and special diet area to the physio department, to the children's ward, to the deep cellars where the sacks of laundry are waiting for collection.

There are cupboards with neatly stacked linen and the hot-water-bottle 'mothers', huge oil-filled containers with thirty or so cylindrical hot-water

The Breaking of the Shell

bottles kept permanently ready at the required temperature. There are sluices which contain stacks of metal bedpans and gas cookers with boiling pans for the sterilizing of needles and syringes as well as tools.

There is the maternity department, with its rows of cots; one operating theatre (the holiest of holies!); and the administration area, where we are to collect our pay packet once a month. And finally there is the mortuary.

My very first visit to the cold mortuary comes after I have spent a day on the ladies' surgical ward. The first corpse I see, to my absolute horror, is that of a kind lady I chatted with and whose pulse and temperature I took only the previous day. Death after surgery is not an unusual occurrence. She lies next to the corpse of a handsome young man who has died in a motorbike accident. On a small table by the door is an enamel bowl, lined with a linen cloth; therein lies a tiny naked baby with spina bifida, the contents of the spine bulging out.

Our day starts at 7.30 a.m., after a Dutch breakfast of bread and cheese, cold meats and jams, and a huge bowl of plain yoghurt—and of course freshly brewed coffee. The dining room is across the road, on the ground floor in the big Victorian villa called Pollenhuis. It is a delightful place full of light and potted plants. All personal notices are pinned on cork notice boards, and our posts can be collected from our pigeonholes, which also contains our napkin in a ring. A clean linen napkin is provided each Sunday morning. Before the new team goes on the ward, we are expected to read the report on each patient, written in thin school exercise books by the outgoing team. The patients will have been awakened at 4 a.m. with a cup of tea and a bowl of hot water by the night staff.

Staff nurses serve breakfast, and all patients are expected to eat whatever is put on a plate for them! A rollicking comes to those who do not clean up their plates, no matter how unwell they are. No food wastage is tolerated. Remember, this is in the days after the war, when shortages are still commonplace and most people will waste nothing in the way of food.

We chart every cup of fluid drunk, every morsel eaten, every bowel movement, every drop of urine passed. Patients' notes are kept under lock and key, and no patient is ever allowed to even glance at them. Not only that, as nurses we are at no time allowed to discuss the patients' own progress, divulge how low or high their temperature is, or anything else. If a patient wishes to know anything at all, she will need to ask the staff nurse, who alone will decide just how much or how little the patient is allowed to know about her own body. All the charts hang at the ends of the beds when the doctors are there but are collected to be put out of sight the very moment they leave the ward.

Beds are made, wounds are dressed, and flowers returned from the corridors where they have spent the night. Water glasses are washed and refreshed.

Thursday is chiropody day, and each patient is treated to a toenail clip and foot wash by the nurses. How they look forward to their foot pampering! Many patients are almost part of the furniture, as they are kept in their beds for weeks or months. So we run a hair-washing service for them as well. Since we do not allow many patients out of bed, doing a hair-wash is a major undertaking, often needing two nurses to cope.

From 10 a.m. onwards the ward is spotless, and the wait for the doctors' round begins. From the very moment the doctors or surgeons arrive on the ward, bedspreads will have been pulled straight many times, patients have been sat up (regardless of how unwell they feel), junior staff have been told to wait outside the ward, any work in progress has to be stopped, and not a pin can be heard to drop. If anyone cleaning bedpans in the sluice room can be heard at all, a dressing down will await them later. Zr Fokker often accompanies the doctors round, and her roving eye will quickly spot anything at all out of place. She knows all the patients, their medical records, where they come from, what their social status might be, who their GPs are, and what their family consists of.

White-coated doctors always come with a silent following. There will be Matron, staff, and the next most senior nurse on the ward. Only the doctor will speak, and he will only address Matron or staff. Doctors do not speak to either patient or junior staff. If the doctor wants to know how well a patient is getting on, he will address Matron, *not* the patient. Doctors and surgeons are treated like earthly gods.

One of the senior surgeons smokes and takes his packet of cigarettes with him into theatre. He sees nothing wrong in smoking while operating on patients.

Being on duty on Sundays is rather special. There is always coffee, strong and freshly brewed. (I never tasted Nescafe coffee till I came to England.) We take a break around 11 a.m., and all the nursing staff sit in a large circle, like a big family, just outside the big swing doors into the ward. Our starched aprons crackle, and everyone is on their best behaviour under the stern scrutiny of staff nurse. Apart from coffee, there is a huge bowl of whipped cream and a plate piled high with cream cakes, a specialty of the Dutch. We are offered the plate according to seniority. But I am always ravenous and take whatever is left on the plate.

We eat a cooked lunch, but on Sunday evening there is always a very large pan of what is known as tonsil soup, on account of the big chunks of fatty beef floating between the egg noodles—these resemble the tonsils removed from small patients! This is a welcome change from bread and jam or cheese. Some senior nurses are allowed to bring their own specialties, such as peanut butter, home-made jams, or vegetarian spreads. Being very junior myself, I will have to wait a few years for that privilege.

Sunday is the one day in the week when we ease up on cleaning the ward. Every other day we clean the doors and windows with blue spirit, polish every surface, and refresh water in each vase of flowers. Cleanliness of the ward is a matter of pride to each of us. We have been lectured on bugs and bacteria ad infinitum.

After coffee, the small portable organ is hoisted onto the long, cumbersome trolley that is used on the wards to move beds. None of the beds have their own wheels, so moving beds is a major operation. Those of us in good voice gather round the small organ, and hymn books are passed around the ward. There is always a nurse who will play the organ. We sing on request for about thirty minutes on each ward, and the patients love it. Some take the trouble to put on their slippers and dressing gowns and move from ward to ward to boost the singing.

Just very occasionally the news that cook has done us a treat is passed round the wards, and it is often first come, first served. If I am finishing off a job on the ward, I am most likely to miss the treat, which might be a crunchy bread roll hollowed out and filled with savoury kidneys, a croquette or a toasted sandwich, a pan of soup or, if we are very lucky, a bowl of home-made pate.

I remember there was one of the nurses who always ate with her head down, stuffing in each mouthful as if it were her last meal. It was only much later that I learned that she, like me, had spent her childhood in Japanese concentration camps. She never forgot that food was the one commodity that mattered, and so she made sure that no one spoke to her, just in case someone would steal her plateful while she was not looking. It was very painful to watch this sad person.

Another nurse, a staff nurse, had one of the fingers missing from her right hand. At that time, syringe needles were always sterilized and reused. After a period of time they became quite blunt and had to be sharpened again! Giving a patient an injection was quite an art when using blunt needles. Each one of us were known for how well or how appallingly we would administer an injection. This particular nurse was known as the torturer of the ward. Her missing finger did not help when she was administering a needle! I would watch her with horror as she almost screwed in the needle. However, she was the kindest person possible and wonderful to the young, green nurses, if quite unaware of the effect she had on patients!

End-of-the-year exams are my nightmare. I work hard at my lectures, am very good at the practical side, and indeed enjoy many privileges given to me for doing responsible work. I have very little trouble learning the medical jargon or procedures, and my exam marks are consistently high. But my self-confidence remains very low. The many years in the camps and with the many foster families have left me with a lack of self-esteem that will haunt me for most of my life.

After many hours of written exams, each of us is interviewed by a panel of doctors, surgeons, staff nurses, and Matron. They all sit behind a very long table, looking very stern and serious. Each asks relevant questions according to their status within the hospital. We wait outside, sitting on a long bench, for our turn to be invited in.

I remember one year, after having been questioned and not getting a single question wrong, that I burst into tears afterwards. I was a bundle of nerves, convinced I had failed. Matron had come out to invite the next victim in for questioning, when she spotted me sniffling away. As she loomed over me, I hastily shot to my feet. I was given a severe reprimand for such ridiculous behaviour and told to pull myself together—at once! We were always reminded who we were, representatives of the hospital, not merely individuals doing our jobs. Being a nurse at Velp involved far more than simply doing my training.

Christmas on the wards is special too. In Holland in the fifties, Christmas does not carry the razzmatazz of later years. Our main winter festival is St Nicolaas, celebrated on 5 December. Presents are exchanged in the evening. Each present is wrapped, and it also contains a poem written to the recipient. The presents all come from St Nicolaas, not from those who have bought the gifts, wrapped them, and written the poem. Often, the longer the poem the smaller the gift.

All gifts are unwrapped and the poems read out amidst much hilarity to all present. It is essentially a festival of fun and giving and receiving. Many gifts are home-made, and always they are tailored to the purse of the giver.

Christmas is celebrated for its religious significance. We share as well a special meal prepared by all the women in the house. There is a Christmas tree with real candles and the same baubles brought out year after year. The only other decoration around the house is fresh greenery and berries brought in from the woods. The children (and even the adults) each receive a book—nothing else, but since all in my family are voracious readers, it is most welcome. Children do not give gifts to parents.

Christmas day in the afternoon is always a peaceful affair as we all quietly dip into our new books and feast on the biscuits and chocolates laid out in big bowls on the coffee table.

In the hospital, Christmas starts at midnight, when all nurses working those days wrap up warmly and start their singing of carols outside the hospital, ensuring that behind each window and door someone will have hear the 'midnight angels.'

The decorations are restrained and very tastefully done, with only fresh greenery from the large gardens around the nurses' Victorian houses. There are lots of candles but none of the brash baubles and glitziness encountered in later years.

Encounter With God

Having grown up in the Christian faith, been baptized in the Dutch Reformed Church, and having lived in a land where different faiths had exposed me to a wide variety of spirituality, I had become aware of the importance of faith in all its different forms. I had from an early age realized that people's emotional responses were often part of their spirituality or faith.

In the camps, where so many people died, many women had found that strength through their faith was the only way to keep going.

The stark contrast between the shocking cruelties of the Japanese and their inability to allow emotions to be seen or shared, and the women's strength in sharing their emotions in the only way they could at that time, demonstrated what our humanity is all about. It is about being part of a community, taking care of each other, sharing losses, food, the tiny personal space, and the care for each other's children, the old, and the infirm. I had watched the young doctor entering the camp afterwards and, on seeing the pathetic remains of my beautiful mother and her three starving children, weep and unashamedly share his emotion.

I have experienced another glimpse into what happens when we allow ourselves to be part of a community or when we learn to let go and let God.

As a very young student nurse, I was asked for the first time to sit with a dying patient. I sat for many hours holding the already-cold hand of my patient, watching the battle between life and death go on. I watched the twitching eyeballs beneath the eyelids, the restless legs, the fidgety hands pulling at the sheets. I saw the final energy trying to hold onto known life and life to come, so unknown to some of us and so certain for others.

I realized the privilege I was experiencing by having a ringside seat at the moment of a human being leaving one world and entering another, the crossing over on the bridge between life and death.

I gradually became aware, in the tiny, spotless, white room, of a presence; a calm presence had entered the room. A great sense of peace had taken hold of my patient as she let go and let God take care of her. There was no great flash of light, no sign of an angel, as we might imagine an angel to be—just this great awareness of God's presence.

My patient died not long after that, while I continued to sit with her for a long time, enclosed in that great balm of peace.

Those of us who have been privileged enough to be present at that mountaintop experience, that certain encounter with God, may know that it might well be the only really close encounter we shall ever have with God.

God sent us His son, and of course it is Jesus's humanity that helps us have that closeness to God, through Jesus's constant presence in our lives, wherever we are on our pilgrimages through life.

Hanneke Coates

WE have to drink our cup slowly,
Tasting every mouthful
All the way to the bottom
Living a complete life is drinking
Our own cup, with its many sorrows,
And joys, claiming it as our
Unique life, then too can we lift
It up for others to see and encourage
Them to lift up our cup
In a fearless gesture,
Proclaiming that we will
Support each other in
Our common journey,
We create a community.

Henri Nouwen

The Breaking Of The Shell 1

In September 1989 I made my first trip back to the country of my birth. It was also the country where my ancestors had made a life as long ago as the early 1700s. They had been the colonizers of a new world; these early pioneers saw it as the ultimate paradise on earth. Many of my ancestors are buried in the volcanic soil covering the slopes of the numerous live volcanoes on the spine of the island of Java.

I wanted to go back to reconnect to where my roots lay, to smell the pungent scent of the tropics, to eat again the exciting spicy food so very different from European fare. I wanted to see if I could still speak the comfortable language again. Most of all, I wanted to be with the beautiful people who live on the archipelago of a thousand islands and whose DNA I share.

The last time I had been there was in 1955. This time I brought my husband and eldest son, Andrew, who had just finished his university degree and was looking for adventure. We hired a car with a driver, called Johannes, who much to my surprise still spoke the language of the Dutch colonizers.

I had planned the route with visits to all the places that lay buried in my memories, including the Soerabaya hospital I had been born in and the small mountainous place called Lembang where my father had tended his plantations. We stayed in the same small hotel where pre-war my grandparents who'd lived in Salatiga had stayed during visits to my family.

We visited the homes I had lived in, the streets I had walked, and the small resort of Tretes, which had been a favourite weekend retreat in the mountains away from the oppressive heat of Soerabaya. We climbed volcanoes and rode horses to almost the top of Mount Bromo, where as a terrified teenager I'd had to be carried to the top in a slendang by two locals. We visited the tiny mountain resort of Kopeng where my parents had honeymooned.

At the home where my grandparents had lived we found the same large red colonial letterbox they would have used. It had been preserved, with all the Dutch times of collection still on its side. We visited their graves and thought about the family that had gathered there for their funerals.

On the spur of the moment, I decided to visit the place of the first concentration camp where as a small child I had been incarcerated with my mother, older sister, and baby brother. It was really no more than curiosity. For almost fifty years we had not spoken about those dark days.

When we'd made our first visit to my mother's family in Holland in 1947, the Dutch had been working hard to begin rebuilding their country after the German occupation. The final winter had been bitterly cold, and food had run out. The Dutch had resorted to eating their tulip bulbs for sustenance. The war in Holland had come to an end by May 1945, but we in the Far East had not been liberated by the English from our hellholes of Japanese concentration camps till August 1945. We'd then remained in the camps for many more months because we had no homes to go to or complete families to begin life again. It was January 1946 when we were finally reunited with our father. We'd then been then plunged almost immediately into the revolution known as the Bersiap time, which brought back independence for the colonies of the Dutch East Indies. This had been the most terrifying time of all, with the Dutch colonials being the most hated people on earth. I recall lying in bed at night listening to the shouts of 'Merdekka' (Freedom) on the streets, hearing the anger in the voices and fearing for the next day without understanding what was going on.

Before I returned to Indonesia in 1989, I had never talked much about the camp years. Memories had been buried so deeply and for so long, and returning to the site of the old camp was just a matter of curiosity. I had no idea what was awaiting me.

The street names I remembered in the cool mountain town of Bandoeng had, of course, been in Dutch. Independence and more than fifty years having passed, the names had been changed or simply translated into *Bahasa Indonesia*, the name for the local language, better known as Malay. Johannes, the driver, soon found *Djalan Angrek* (Orchid Street); it was still there. The three-bedroom number 17 bungalow that we had been squeezed into along with a hundred other housemates was still there. It did not bear much resemblance to the filthy, squalid area of the camp years.

The Catholic mission, once the perimeter of the camp that had housed six thousand woman and children, was still there too. And there, lo and behold, was the parade ground. I felt confused, as the Nissen huts were still there and the barbed wire still around the parade ground. And there were soldiers wearing khaki uniforms. Nothing had changed! At the end of the concrete apron stood the tall, ancient kapok tree that had all those years ago been the scene of the stringing up of two young Dutch East Indies soldiers. They had been fathers of children in the camp who had come to say their farewell before being taken off to work on the Burma railway but had been cruelly punished by the Nippon for doing so.

I experienced a deep sense of grief that kept coming and coming, completely overwhelming me. I began to weep, but had you asked me what I was weeping about I could not have told you. That night I cried for four or five hours, and I had no idea what it was about. It did not bring relief but just confused me. It was only recently, when Andrew and I were reminiscing about that trip, that Andrew told me that after that day I did not speak for three whole days. I have no memory of that at all.

It was the beginning of the breaking of the shell.

As a family we never talked much about our war experiences. The war in Europe had finished long before the war in the Far East, and we had not returned to Holland till 1947.

The Dutch had by May 1945 turned a corner and were trying to begin anew and forget about the war years. They had not really wanted to hear much about the concentration camps we had been in, or the Burma railway my father had worked on, or his years of slave labour for the Nippon in Osaka in a copper manufacturing factory.

In reality, we did not start talking about those times for fifty years. People like my father never spoke about those years at all. It was simply a no-go area.

The Dutch in Holland, too, had suffered horrendously, having been occupied by the Germans. The two last winters had been bitter, with all the trees chopped down for firewood, the only heating or wood for cooking.

They, too, had starved that final winter. Many of them had wanted also to forget those years.

When we tried to speak about our horror years our Dutch family remarked that we could not possibly have suffered as much as they had. After all we had lived all those years in a nice warm country.

After our return to Holland, we had been given a small extra ration of sugar, and my mother's brother, Oom Jan, had been positively disgusted as he considered us rich spoiled colonials who did not deserve anything special, least of all sugar.

When the Americans dropped the first nuclear bomb on Hiroshima, as a warning to the Japanese that this was only the beginning of the end for them, the Japanese did not believe them. They refused to surrender and played every trick in the book to stall capitulation. They did not even tell their own people about the annihilation of Hiroshima. Days later a second bomb evaporated the city of Nagasaki.

Around the world, the second bomb has always been a hot topic of debate. It should not have happened. It was a crime against humanity. Why could the Hiroshima bomb not have sufficed? and so on. Very few people know that the emperor of Japan, Hirohito himself, had already signed and distributed a leaflet for all his hundreds of thousands of soldiers. It ordered them never to surrender. At that time, the emperor was seen to be a god, and it was bred into the Japanese to obey his instruction without question. The leaflet gave a long list of how to dispose of all POWs, women and children as well as Allied soldiers, held captive in the hundreds of camps around Asia.

These are some of the methods preferred: decapitating us, cutting out our hearts while alive, drowning us, burying us alive en masse, shooting us, and poisoning us. These are just some of the methods the Japanese soldiers were instructed to dispatch us with. However, it did say at the end of the leaflet that *any* method of murder would have been preferable to surrender. This was to happen to millions of POWs around the Far East

I see my own family now, my children with their own children, and I know with certainty that without Nagasaki they would not be around today. I would have perished, along with all those others.

That does not make it any easier to come to terms with the annihilation of so many other innocents. I know now that reconciliation, forgiveness, and peace are the only way forward.

The Breaking of the Shell

If you can remember that you are
a child of God and very precious,
If you can remember to let go and let God,
If you can forgive those that have abused you
and leave those hurts at the foot of the cross,
Then you will walk in the light and
leave the shadows behind you.
Life is God's gift to you,
What you do with that gift
is your gift to God

H C.

Ambassadors For Reconcilliation

After we returned from our trip to Java, with the disastrous effect the return to the concentration camp site had had on me, I became deeply depressed. By nature a sanguine person, I had never known such a feeling of darkness and hopelessness. Each day brought bleakness and the utter feeling of failure.

I did not understand where it was coming from. In the beginning I did not connect it to those dark days of concentration camps or my teenage years in the loveless foster families. In all my years in England I never met another person who knew about the Far Eastern concentration camps, so I could not share my memories.

I had married an Englishman in 1963. My marriage lasted for 40 years.

My 3 children, two boys and a girl were born within 3 ½ years of each other and I was very content to take care of my family for many years.

My husband was the real Alpha male, always right, always controlling and a great one for organising everything connected to family life. He also had a fierce temper. and had become physically abusive as well as verbally. Broken bones and bruises were regularly part of my life. He was always critical of anything I did that did not fit in with the norm or anything I did that put me on a pedestal above him. I was often told how stupid I was.

Domestic abuse was not recognised or talked about in those days.

My life had become a daily emotional battering and I did not know how to deal with it

I desperately wanted to return to nursing, but soon realised that was not part of his plan for me.

However Hospiscare was something new in those days and I had always been interested in end of life care so was asked by our local GP to run our local district Hospiscare. I went to conferences, took courses and passed on my knowledge to the team of volunteers I was in charge of in10 week training sessions.

This was a voluntary job so I was able to and always very careful to run the day to day Hospiscare business during my own home hours that did not interfere with meal times or family times.

I had always been able to cope with the dark side of my marriage by forgiving and forgetting. There were few people with whom I could share what I was going through, mostly on account of my desperate need to conform, fit in, and be seen as the good wife of a man who was such a cog in the village and such a pillar of the church community.

In our lifetime journeys we all make friends, and meet strangers. We are not always aware of the healing effect our caring has on people. Those strangers or friends may also understand things about us which we have never recognised ourselves.

It is as Henri Nouwen the Dutch Theologian and writer tells us,: caring is part of being a community.

We all yearn for love and long to be understood. When Jesus joins us on our journeys of life, bit by bit, God's presence in our world is revealed to us.

We ourselves, along with those who have been there for us, if only in a brief encounter, become part of the story of redemption and forgiveness.

One of the early people who put her finger on my trauma's was Louise, a young Police officer who came to visit me the day after my husband had walked out on me.

She had been tipped off by the Hospital Doctor who had diagnosed the broken bones and had recognised the domestic abuse which had been the cause of it.

It was Louise who quickly realised that it was through my early years of abuse in the camps that I had become the person who needed to do as she had been told without rebelling or disobeying It was Louise who for the first time coined together the words " you have from your early years in the camps been conditioned to be humiliated.

Our vicar, Deryck, and his wife, Margaret, were two people who had a healing effect on me. They knew what was going on in my home and would always have time to pray and listen. This was a friendship that accepted me for who I was and believed me, however unbelievable my sad stories of my home life must have appeared to them. They saw through the made-up stories about a game with the dog gone wrong to explain the bruises or the operation on a fractured eye socket. They, too, were rooted in the love of Jesus and God's presence in the world. They taught me to continue to trust and obey; and that in the end all would be well—all would be well.

Then there was Ruth, the head teacher of our village school. She, too, guessed what was going on but would never pry. She often would come to see me, just hold my hand, and repeat again and again, 'Just keep remembering that you are a child of God and very precious. You *are* very precious.'

After almost two years of deep depression and a fractured home life, I was in the High Street one day and met up with Rita, an elderly lady from the Methodist Church. She had spent a lifetime battling depression, which I had been unaware of. I told her how I felt and that I had lost my faith, being unable to pray or come to church. This is what she said to me: 'It does not matter that you cannot pray now. God knows that. We are all praying for you, and it is God himself who is praying for you.'

That was the day that I crossed the River Rubicon.

On Joy and Sorrow

> Then a woman said, 'Speak to us on joy and sorrow.'
> Your joy is your sorrow unmasked.
> And the self same well from which your laughter rises was oftentimes filled with your tears.
> How else can it be?
> The deeper that sorrow carves into your being, the more joy you can contain.
> Is not the cup that holds your wine the very cup that was burned in the potter's oven?
> And is not the lute that soothes your spirit the very wood that was hollowed with knives?
> When you are joyous, look deep into your heart, and you shall find it is only that which has given you sorrow that is giving you joy.
> When you are sorrowful, look again in your heart, and you shall see that in truth you are weeping for that which has been your delight.
> Some of you say, 'Joy is greater than sorrow,' and others say, 'Nay, sorrow is the greater.'
> But I say unto you, they are inseparable.
> Together they come, and when one sits alone with you at your board, remember that the other is asleep upon your bed.
> Verily you are suspended like scales between your sorrow and your joy.
> Only when you are empty are you at standstill and balanced.
> When the treasure-keeper lifts you to weigh his gold and silver, needs must your joy or your sorrow rise or fall.

—Khalil Gibran

Crossing The River Rubicon

Returning my life to normality was a slow process, and I felt I was almost leaving my family behind. They had no idea what I had been going through and assumed that much of my depression was of my own making. So the subject was never spoken about. Deep within me there was a perception that this was a rather disgraceful part of my life.

Having crossed the river of no return, I felt my faith deepening, but much of it was lived almost in secrecy.

My husband had left me after forty years of marriage. After the initial shock of such humiliation, it took me very little time to realize that suddenly I had the freedom to do what I wanted, without being in the constant state of nerves I had been in for so long. I had always played the obliging partner, always on the lookout to please and obey.

It was as if suddenly an oxygen mask had been put on my face. All I had to do was breath it in.

I began to realize that if I wanted to live a life of freedom I would need to put the past behind me. I would begin by forgiving my partner for all the years of humiliation, bullying, and domestic abuse.

I spent five days at Lee Abbey, in North Devon. This is a Christian retreat centre, where I was to follow a course for those going through divorce or breakdown of a relationship. There were eighty other participants there, and the sheer numbers encouraged me to realize that there were other people going through the same thing. I was not alone!

I was able for the first time to talk about my feelings and be listened to and understood—without being criticized or lectured to. It was also the first time I acknowledged and spoke about domestic abuse.

A lot of the course was made up of sensible and practical advice. For example, if you want to take a first step towards forgiveness, write a short letter. Simply say that you are sorry about the breakup and anything you contributed to it and that you would like to forgive all that has passed. Do not go into detail, and leave it at that.

It was an empowering experience.

The breakup of a relationship can leave a person very lonely. Who can you trust to go to? How many of those you share your story with will believe you? Will they accept your side of the story, especially if your partner has always been a popular and big contributor to the church, society, and local community? There were those who admired your 'perfect' family life when those dark days were well hidden behind doors for so long. None of us know what does go on behind people's front doors.

In the early years of the new millennium, domestic abuse was not a subject much understood or spoken about. I struggled for years afterwards to deal with those who would ask me quite seriously, 'What did you do to him for him to leave you?'

The exciting thing happening to me was that for the first time in my life I began to realize that there was a whole new person emerging from years of pretence, an altogether other person that had been suppressed, bullied, and dominated for years. My natural gifts had been abused or kicked into the grass for years. I was not the stupid person I had been made to believe I was. As a child I had always enjoyed painting and drawing but had abandoned my talents when I realized that these skills were only encouraged for the benefit of producing endless posters and other 'useful' products. The results had always been openly criticized until they fit the right criteria. Nothing had ever been praised but had been part of the controlling atmosphere I'd lived in. Now I found solace in the quiet days creating wild-flower watercolours and felt the joy of being creative and producing something I loved.

I enjoyed being on my own and realized that at heart I am an introvert, not the jolly extroverted person who had fitted the profile of the wife of the man who was that extravert. The real me liked to take care of the dogs, sheep, geese, and chickens I surrounded myself with. I craved the solace, silence, and peace of the farmstead.

I had made progress in digging into my early years, and writing my stories down turned out to be a cathartic, healing exercise. I began to realize that what had happened to me all those years ago in the camps and during my teenage years was at the root of my constant need to conform to be acceptable. I began to realize that here, too, was an opportunity for forgiveness. And so began the next part of my journey of forgiveness.

Step By Step

For a long time I had been pondering the words of the police woman Louise who had come to see me at home. This was after I'd learned that I had four broken ribs and my sternum as a result of the final assault on me before my husband had walked out and left me. She had listened to my story and told me that I fitted the profile of a domestic abuse victim exactly, and all this was because I had been *conditioned* to be humiliated from the very early days in my life at the hands of the Japanese soldiers.

I had already begun to dig deep into my childhood memories. Some of them were my mother's stories as she had told them to me when I had questioned her about those days. My own memories went back a very long way, as I realized when writing them down and recalling in great detail the minutia of the emotions that had assaulted me. I remembered even the print on the cloth of the dress my mother had been wearing at particular events, the smell of the mat I slept on, or the exact layout of the crowded houses we lived in during the war years.

The events concerning my early years always came back to the Japanese soldiers. How does one begin to forgive people who have done such atrocious things to a small child—and thus, as I now know, to my parents, my siblings, and my entire family? And who knows have had an effect on second and third generations.

Their actions have had such a profound backlash for so many years.

Today I go into churches, schools, secular group meetings, and universities to tell them my story of forgiveness. The question is the same wherever I speak: 'How can you forgive when people have committed such atrocities to other human beings, especially small children?'

As Christians, we hold forgiveness and love at the heart of our faith, and I realized that when I began my journey into those dark days. I somehow needed to find the courage, the faith, and belief in doing the right thing. I learned very early on that if we want to forgive, we must realize that forgiveness is not about our perpetrators.

Forgiveness is about ourselves and our willingness to forgive

It is about God's grace within us and our hearts.

It is a heart thing.

Life is made up of the decisions we make. Forgiveness is one of those decisions. It says in John 20–23 that if we forgive people's sins, they are forgiven. If we do not forgive them, they are not forgiven.

So here is the stark choice. If we allow room in our lives for unforgiveness, then we will also make room for a great deal of negativity. A foothold will become a stronghold.

So, what do we do with other people's sins that have so affected us all through life? When we forgive someone, or for that matter an entire nation, like the Japanese, we also have to face our own resentment first. We must try to find some buried emotions first. It helps to make a list of things that have hurt us most, such as anger, lies, humiliation, broken trust, cruelty, bullying, controlling attitudes, physical assaults, etc.

When we forgive someone, we have to be quite specific about what has been done to us. We must not take on the blame ourselves for what others have done to us.

Throughout my marriage I always felt guilty. I felt I was a failure, and I spent a lifetime trying to fit in, mainly because I was not allowed to talk about my feelings. But the lack of communication was not *my* failure. My need to communicate was treated with derision.

Once we have made the choice to forgive someone, we will need to allow our emotions to catch up. We must not expect to feel constant relief for having forgiven! Forgiveness is a long journey, and we need all our courage to follow it to the end. We must also be intentional about where we direct our energy. Keeping score of those who have wronged us will ultimately destroy us, not the wrongdoers. The Japanese soldiers who had so affected the rest of my life were most likely all dead by this point, so I had no one to hold to account. In some ways this made forgiveness of the Japanese soldiers easier. But if those who have wronged us can been seen living a life of luxury and success, or being put on a pedestal for charitable deeds and even publicly denounce their guilt, it will be hard to be a forgiving person.

However, forgiveness is always the better choice than un forgiveness.

The Japanese as a nation have until very recently buried their history of atrocities. And yet the whole world knows about Hiroshima and Nagasaki, and their suffering as a result of those deeds has been mourned around the world. People from far and wide make pilgrimages to Hiroshima or Nagasaki.

In the Dutch East Indies alone the Japanese army had set up three hundred so called protection camps for the Europeans living on the islands, which quickly became concentration camps. Very few people even today know what went on in those numerous concentration or POW camps. Our Allied soldiers who ended up on the Burma railway or POW camps are even today referred to as 'The forgotten army'. My journey of forgiveness had all those different aspects woven into the fabric of forgiveness.

Love and forgiveness are closely linked. Neither manifests itself in a one-off meal ticket. A marriage certificate does not ensure undying love for the other half. We have to work at loving on a daily basis. So it is also with forgiveness.

While the sun shines it may be easy to forgive those who have sinned against us. But on another day, resentment may come out of the woodwork, and forgiveness will be far removed from our hearts. This is alright and all part of our long journey of forgiveness.

But we need to work at forgiveness on a daily basis.

It is important that we learn not to blame the past for the present. God will have been hard at work in us, removing, restoring, and revealing things in our lives. So we must learn to let go and let God deal with certain parts of our lives.

When we forgive, we release peace and restoration to the forgiven person(s) as well as to ourselves. In some cases, it may be helpful to make a clean break with those who have hurt us, as I did with the father of my children. I knew that if I did not, my life would always be controlled by him in one form or another.

The most important message about forgiveness is to understand that forgiveness begins with *you*. It begins in your heart. That is where the changes take place.

As Christians, we know that when we begin our journey of forgiveness, God will be working within us, changing us and helping us to deal with those changes from hatred to love.

Forgiveness is not about our perpetrators, although the perpetrators may well see what is happening to us and therefore change too. Many of the forgiveness stories at the Forgiveness Project will testify as to what can unexpectedly happen when one person starts the journey of forgiveness.

I had made my journey and thought that I had reached the point at which I could truly say I had let go of hatred and had forgiven the Japanese people. Then, in 2011, the world awoke to the news that Japan had been devastated by a huge tsunami. For many weeks we watched on our TVs or listened to our radios about a nation devastated. I recall seeing tiny, traumatized children and little old ladies numbed into shock on television. I saw schoolchildren who were bereft of everything. Then Japanese journalists would come on the screen and tell us about the number unaccounted for, the thousands who had died, the thousands left homeless. The cameras would show us towns and villages destroyed and lives turned upside down.

I had soon realized that each time I heard a Japanese voice I became unsettled, and the hairs on the back of my neck rose. I slowly began to understand that I had not let go of all my negative feelings towards the Japanese people. I had not truly forgiven, and I had no idea how to deal with it.

The following Sunday when I went to church, our vicar told us of a collection that would be held in aid of the Japanese, and she pleaded with us to 'dig deep'. I remember repeatedly thinking, *Dig deep for the Japanese! Dig deep for the Japanese?*

In the end I did what I usually do when I do not know how to cope. I prayed and asked God to deal with it, as I did not know how to. I then let it go.

People say that God works in mysterious ways, and indeed He does. Without thinking much more about it, I did dig deep the following Sunday.

I have never been plagued since by Japanese voices.

Reconcilliation And Forgiveness

In April 2015 I learned through an article in my paper that during the month of September, exactly seventy years after the liberation of the POW camps in Japan, there would be an unveiling ceremony for a memorial at the site of a former camp just outside Nagasaki.

There was an appeal to survivors or members of the POW soldiers' families from that camp to consider joining them for the unveiling. Without much hesitation I emailed the paper to tell them that I was a survivor of one of the Japanese camps and that my father had been on the Burma–Thai railway and also been a POW in Japan. I asked if they could please tell me more.

Within an hour I had an email back from the Tokyo journalist attached to the paper, promising to put me in touch with the organizers. Yoshiko Tamura's reply came very shortly afterwards, and so began my final journey of reconciliation and forgiveness with the Japanese people.

My son Andrew had managed to find my father's war record on the internet. Some of the information was in Dutch and Malay, but most of the information was, of course, in Japanese. My father and I had spoken so little about the war years that I realized that some of what I thought I knew might well be incorrect. I had always been under the impression that my father had been somewhere near Nagasaki when the bomb was dropped. Yoshiko quickly realized from reading his records that this was not so, but it somehow did not matter.

My journey was as much about making my peace with the Japanese people as locating the camp site where my father had spent the final war years. His spirit would undoubtedly be there with us. My two sons, Andrew and James, and James's 11 year-old son, Joshua, decided to join me. We went ahead with booking our flight.

I have to confess to being absolutely terrified at meeting the Japanese. To visit the land of the rising sun whose flag and emperor I had bowed to daily while in captivity over so many years seemed an unlikely final step of my journey. I had no idea how I was going to react or what I was letting myself in for. My memories of the Japanese soldiers were of screaming, angry, patronizing, whip-wielding, controlling, cruel men.

Throughout the long journey I fretted over how I was going to deal with meeting my former jailers. I had come to extend my hand in reconciliation and forgiveness, and even friendship. Indeed, I had already walked the path of forgiveness for a long time. This final part of the journey would undoubtedly test my faithfulness. But sometimes we must venture into the darkest rooms of our house and search certain corners of the subconscious to find our peace. That darkness often turns out to be the place where we find the light more brilliant than all the little lamps, the tiny fireflies, or the bright stars that have lit up the night skies to show us the path before. I unexpectedly recall my night of sitting with a dying patient. And it is in these unexpected corners of our houses that we then find the mysterious light of all peace to enter our hearts.

I need not have worried. The Japanese people that I met and those who had organized the memorial site were courteous, soft-spoken, gentle, and so very generous. They were full of remorse for what their nation had done to my family.

Touching their foreheads with both hands, they bowed their heads and repeated again and again how sorry they were for all that their people had done to me and my family. It was the very first time anyone had ever shown me remorse and told me that what we had been through had actually happened and someone was truly sorry!

The Japanese nation has never acknowledged their guilt for the part they played in WWII. A lot of their war history has simply been wiped from the records. Whole generations have grown up unaware of what their nation did to so many innocents.

But there is a remarkable group of people who have acknowledged these facts and now spend all their time researching old POW camp sites, restoring graves or cremation sites, collecting ashes, and reburying them with full honours and sensitive services. They are researching all the names of those who worked under such appalling conditions and those who died from malnutrition, accidents on site, tropical diseases, or simply exhaustion. They have put up commemorative plagues where POW camps once existed.

Most importantly, they are translating wartime records (now available to anyone on the internet) for the families mourning the loss of those who died or those that did not know what had happened to their loved ones. Or they are simply filling in the gaps in the lives of those men who never spoke about their years in captivity. They bring some sense of peace and understanding to their families. It is often second and even third generations that now make these journeys, to enable them to make peace with themselves as well as the new generations of the Japanese soldiers who ruled our camps.

The researchers raise their own funds, set up dialogue days with relatives, and travel across the world to speak to different nations, while taking on board much of the anger or resentment that is still simmering.

They were interested in my father's entries in his small bible, as it confirmed the dates of earthquakes and floods and alarms that had sounded towards the end of the war, when American bombers had started to fly over. But they could not make much sense of the locations my father had noted, until I read them out for them, pronouncing them the Dutch way. It was only then that we realized my father had written them down phonetically as, of course, he had only heard the spoken version of locations. Very soon they were able to tell us details of his long and painful journey throughout the war.

As I slowly dropped my defences, the Japanese remained courteous and treated us to some very generous hospitality.

The most profound change came over me when I visited the Nagasaki bomb museum and stood at the epicentre of where the bomb had been dropped. Seeing the huge black-and-white photographs of total destruction, annihilation, dust, and nothingness, I realized just what it is that war does to people. The ordinary people of Nagasaki had been innocent also.

On the day the memorial was unveiled, we were introduced to British, Dutch, Australian, and American ambassadors all representing their countries, ourselves, and the men who had been imprisoned all those years ago. There were local dignitaries, Japan's Foreign Affairs representatives, and many more. There were representatives of different religious denominations: Buddhist, Shinto, Christians, and even a group of Japanese Christians working under the name Agape.

I had discovered that Nagasaki has for a very long time had a thriving Christian community, going back to the 1700 when the first Dutch missionaries entered the Nagasaki harbour. Ironically, one of the buildings that was entirely destroyed in the nuclear blast of the H-bomb was the large Roman Catholic cathedral.

Today a secondary school stands on the site of the camp, and throughout the ceremony the schoolchildren's orchestra played for us, reducing many of us to tears when they played 'Amazing Grace' while small black swallowtail butterflies gently fluttered among us and settled on our clothing. It had been a long and emotional day for all of us.

Nothing would ever be the same again.

O Lord,

    Remember not only the men and women of goodwill, but also those of ill will.
    But do not remember the suffering they have inflicted upon us;
    Remember the fruits we brought thanks to this suffering,
    Our comradeship, our loyalty, our humility, the courage, the generosity, the greatness of heart
    which has grown out of this;
    And when they come to judgement,
    Let all the fruits that we have born [sic] be their forgiveness.

    This prayer was found beside a dead child in Ravensbrück concentration camp in Germany.

Johanna Albertha Hoorn_Aergelo

Born 26 September 1912, died 2 September 1996

Here follows a short history of my mammie, who travelled around the world most of her life yet died in the country she was born in and is buried in the Hooge Vuursche Dutch Reformed Church yard just opposite the Royal Palace De Draekenberg.

Born in Amersfoort, Holland, an ancient town full of canals and bridges, Jo (or Jootje, to my father) was the eldest daughter of Geerlig Karel Aergelo and Johanna Alberta Aergelo-de Valk. Her brother, Jan Karel and sister, Lena, followed not long after.

Jo became a Montessori infant teacher and spent her first working years in Limburg in the south of Holland. She met Niek, my father, while he was studying tropical agriculture at the Deventer College. They soon fell in love, and she became a globetrotter, following him to Java, where he had his first job as a tea planter in Lembang, Central Java.

She came out by ship from Holland all by herself, having married Niek 'by glove'. This strange arrangement meant that she could travel the six-week-long journey without a chaperone because she was legally a married woman. In those days it was common practice for young brides to come out to the colonies chaperoned. But the 'by glove' ceremony meant she could travel as an 'attached' young woman. A proper marriage ceremony was held shortly after her arrival, on 17 January 1938, in Kedoeng Pring, mid Java.

It was when she was expecting her third baby that she moved voluntarily into what the Japanese called 'protection camps' but which soon became imprisonment. Having lived a relatively privileged life both in Holland and the Dutch East Indies, she soon learned that life in a concentration camp with three small children would require more than toughness and survival skills. She was a real Dutch woman, without sentimentality and possessing a down-to-earth attitude to life and a great loyalty to husband and children. Typically of her generation, she displayed a complex mixture of deeply compassionate and at times almost mercenary attitude for her fellow beings.

She was quite unashamedly racist most of her life, although she softened towards the final years. Inexplicably, she then gave most generously to third-world countries and became quite emotional at seeing injustice done to those of different colour.

Having married into a mixed-race family, and as did the mixed-race families in the Far East during that era, she would refer to the *other* mixed raced families as 'Indos'. Like many Dutch people, she called a spade a spade and was embarrassingly outspoken.

I recall a shopping trip in Amsterdam when I was at the awkward age of 16. We were in a large department store when she asked whether I needed anything. I plucked up courage and wondered if I could buy some deodorant, a fairly new fangled idea in the fifties. To my acute and everlasting embarrassment, she questioned me in a loud voice for the whole store to hear: 'What do you want that for? Do you stink?'

But she was the most generous person I know. If anyone coming into her home would admire anything at all, she would whip it off the wall and instantly present the admirer with it, regardless of its value. The years in the camps had made her realize that possessions were only possessions, not of any real value.

A most gifted person, she always had something in her hands: sewing, knitting, embroidery, or tapestry work. She was a wonderful seamstress and made new birthday frocks for the girls each year. I remember standing blindfolded on a chair (so that the new frock would be a great surprise on the big day) to have the hem pinned in the right place. She would embroider my dresses with flowers of every hue all along the bottom. She loved her garden and would work till dark.

With all of her four children and most of the rest of her family at the other end of the world, she was a copious letter writer. She loved life and lived it fully. She was perfectly content to live all over the world, from the Far East, to Europe, to West and South Africa. She spent lengthy holidays in Australia and New Zealand, visiting her scattered children and grandchildren. In those days travel was still quite cumbersome. It would take forty-eight hours to fly from Indonesia to Holland, stopping off somewhere en route to be put up in a nice hotel for a good night's sleep. She travelled extensively by herself and only in the final years of her life gave up her nomadic life.

It annoyed her immensely that all her eight grandchildren were English speaking, and on more than one occasion she picked a fight with me for not teaching my children to speak Dutch. She spoke fluent Bahasa-Indonesia and English.

She embraced widowhood with true Dutch get-on-with-it attitude, filling her life with hobbies and corresponding with her ever-increasing family around the world. She would never forget a birthday or wedding day. She sent St Nicolaas parcels to all the children and grandchildren each year, almost till the end. With typical Dutch hospitality, she kept open house, displaying great loyalty to old camp friends and childhood friends.

Towards the end of her life she became almost entirely blind and unable to do any of the hobbies that had kept her going for more than twenty years of widowhood. She never grumbled or complained while she patiently waited for the end to come, in the sure knowledge that she would be reunited with Niek in heaven.

I owe all of my life to her, for her stoicism, faith, optimism, hard work, and—most of all—her unstinting love. She was one of those rare women who went into a concentration camp with two children and came out with three, giving birth to my brother in the camp. Many children died in the camps, but somehow she managed to keep us all alive.

Jules Nocolaas Hoorn, Known As Niek

Born 6 December 1911, died 21 June 1973

Niek Hoorn 1940

My pappie was born in Semarang, Java, Dutch East Indies. He is buried together with his wife at De Lage Vuursche, near Utrecht in Holland. He was given the name Nicolaas because his birth occurred the day after the Dutch Saint Nicolaas festival.

Niek was the fourth child of Arnoldus Franciscus Hoorn (Frans) and Berendina Jacoba (Koos), nee Levasier. His oldest brother was Eddy, his sister Mercedes, known as Mary and his youngest brother Adri. Adri died from tetanus infection at the early age of 13. Niek would often recall his brother's tragic death, which had a profound effect on him.

The family owned a pony and trap, which were kept in the outbuildings. Adri contracted tetanus after playing near the dung heap. The funeral was held on the same day as the death occurred. In the tropics, in those early days without refrigeration, it would have been too hot to allow a body to remain above the ground for any length of time.

Adri had been an outstanding young musician, and my father would recall how Adri could play the piano at such a high standard that people would come past the house for a stroll in the early evening just to enjoy this young boy's playing.

My parents met in Deventer when Pappie spent three years at the famous School for Tropical Agricultural. He had never been to Holland or anywhere else in Europe before, so this experience was quite a culture shock. He and my mammie met at one of the many college dances. To this day the college is referred to as Deventer, rather as the English refer to Cirencester. The Agriculture College (now a University)

All prospective planters went to Deventer. the town where the college is.

After Deventer, my father returned to the Far East, leaving my mother to continue her teaching job in Limburg, in the far south of Holland, till 1938. She travelled alone to Java, and they were married on 17 January 1938, in Kedoeng Pring, mid Java.

Niek became a tea planter in the hills of Lembang, mid Java.

This flyer (dropped by B-29 American bombers, the same aircraft that dropped the Hiroshima and Nagasaki bombs) was found by my sister Heleen among a file of wartime correspondence. It must have been the first news the POWs received to tell them that the Far East war was finally over. I passed a copy on to the research team in Nagasaki. They had never seen it. Such precious information would have been treasured by the men and not shared with the Japanese.

レンゴウグンホリョヘ
ALLIED PRISONERS

The JAPANESE Government has surrendered. You will be evacuated by ALLIED NATIONS forces as soon as possible.

Until that time your present supplies will be augmented by air-drop of U.S. food, clothing and medicines. The first drop of these items will arrive within one (1) or two (2) hours.

Clothing will be dropped in standard packs for units of 50 or 500 men. Bundle markings, contents and allowances per man are as follows:

BUNDLE MARKINGS

50 MAN PACK	500 MAN PACK	CONTENTS	ALLOWANCES PER MAN	50 MAN PACK	500 MAN PACK	CONTENTS	ALLOWANCES PER MAN
A	3	Drawers	2	B	10	Laces, shoe	1
A	1-2	Undershirt	2	A	11	Kit, sewing	1
B	22	Socks (pr)	2	C	31	Soap, toilet	1
A	4-6	Shirt	1	C	4-6	Razor	1
A	7-9	Trousers	1	C	4-6	Blades, razor	10
C	23-30	Jacket, field	1	C	10	Brush, tooth	1
A	10	Belt, web, waist	1	B	31	Paste, tooth	1
A	11	Capt, H.B.T.	1	C	10	Comb	1
B	12-21	Shoes (pr)	1	B	32	Shaving cream	1
A	1-2	Handkerchiefs	3	C	12-21	Powder(insecticide)	1
C	32-34	Towel	1				

There will be instructions with the food and medicine for their use and distribution.

C A U T I O N

DO NOT OVEREAT OR OVERMEDICATE   FOLLOW DIRECTIONS

INSTRUCTIONS FOR FEEDING 100 MEN

To feed 100 men for the first three (3) days, the following blocks (individual bundles dropped) will be assembled:

3 Blocks No. 1
(Each Contains)

2 Cases Soup, Can
1 Cases Fruit Juice
1 Case Accessory Pack

1 Block No. 5
(Each Contains)

1 Case Soup, Dehd
1 Case Veg Puree
1 Case Bouillon
1 Case Hosp Supplies
1 Case Vitamin Tablets

1 Block No. 3
(Each Contains)

1 Case Candy
1 Case Gum
1 Case Cigarettes
1 Case Matches

3 Blocks No. 2
(Each Contains)

3 Cases "C" Rations
1 Case Hosp Supplies
2 Cases Fruit

1 Block No. 7
(Each Contains)

1 Case Nescafe
1 Sack Sugar
1 Case Milk
1 Case Cocoa

1 Block No. 10
(Each Contains)

3 Cases Fruit
2 Cases Juice

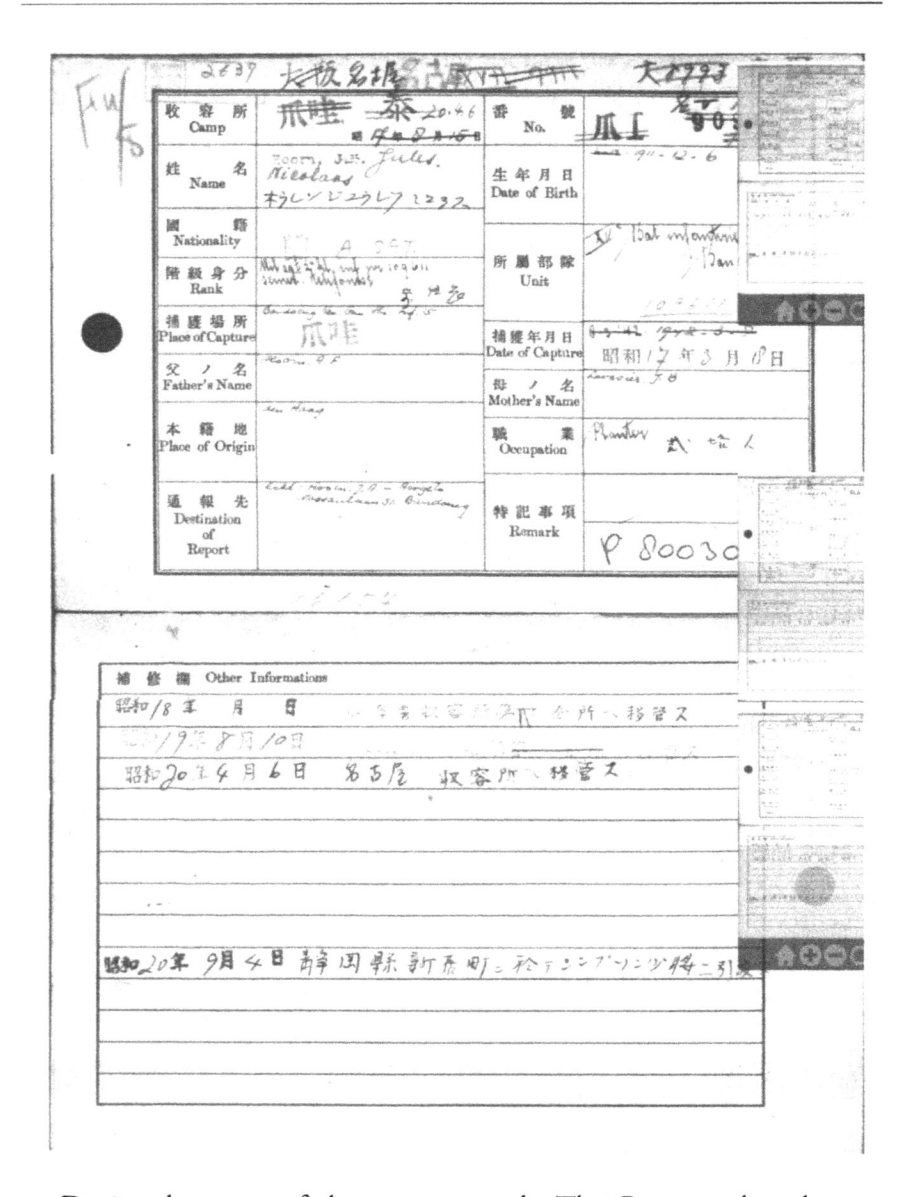

During the war my father was sent to the Thai Burma railway line and put to work on the bridge over the river Kwai. However, at one stage of his time working on the railway he became malnourished and unwell with the usual tropical diseases that affected all POWs. He also suffered from wounds and sores that would not heal. One night he was left to die, lying by the side of the railway, rather than be carried back to camp. The Japanese officer considered he was not worth the haul back to camp, as he was simply going to die anyway.

He expected the wild animals would probably finish him off.

During the night he was found by local Thais who lived in the jungle. They carried him away into their home. This was, of course, a very dangerous thing for them to do. If they had been found harbouring a prisoner, it would have spelled certain death for them. They cared for him and dressed his wounds, and when he had sufficiently recovered they let him go back into the jungle. Not long afterwards he was recaptured by the Nippon.

After the completion of the railway, he spent time at Camp Rivers, near Singapore, before he was shipped out to Japan on one of their death ships. Large numbers of POWs were put into the hold of the ship with almost no facilities; they would stop off at Formosa (now Taiwan). Many POWs died on those long journeys. My father was then taken to Osaka, at Nagoya No. 6 Camp, where he worked at a munitions factory, making copper components for bullets that would kill our own people.

One of the rare stories that he would tell about his time spent in Japan was as follows. Among the Dutch POWs was one man who had been a scientist before the war. He managed to secretly change the copper components to a much softer consistency. It was many months before the Japanese found out that the bullets they had been supplying their soldiers with were as good as useless! Severe punishment for the entire camp followed, but they all agreed it had been worth it!

Pappie rarely spoke about his experiences. I do know that he carried a small bible with him, which gave him a great deal of comfort. My brother now owns that bible, and the entries in the back have been of great interest to the Japanese, as they have been able to compare dates with existing dates of earthquakes and floods.

I never saw my father wear a wedding ring; he had sold it during the war in return for a loaf of bread. He was a difficult man to get to know and, especially after retirement, would often moodily sit and stare out of the big Dutch windows for days on end, smoking one cigarette after another in total silence, neither speaking nor answering questions. He would suddenly get up, put his coat on, and without saying anything, catch the train to Amsterdam and not return till late in the day.

As small children after the war, when we became too noisy we were often sent away to the blakan, the outbuildings where the servants lived. Our father was impatient with too many children around him and rarely showed much affection. He was a man of few words.

He was the most handsome man I know, his dark skin revealing his Malaysian DNA. He dressed immaculately. After the war he worked for the BAT (British American Tobacco company).

I adored him and was quite in awe of him despite his lack of closeness. But I well remember the tears in my eyes when I was rebuked for my clumsiness, my appalling shyness and, worse still, my complete lack of refined ladylikeness.

He had a genuine horror at my fascination with creepy crawlies, snakes, bats, and birds. He could not understand my pleasure at these creatures, as they might bite, and a bite in the tropics could well spell death. His anger at my 'stupidity' was unconcealed.

The camp years took their toll later in his life, although I am quite certain he would not have recognized his depressions as a result of the war years.

His mother, Jacoba (Koosje for short) Levasier, came from a French Huguenot family that had settled in Holland after the French Revolution.

His father, Franciscus, was a half-blood, having been born into a large, noisy, happy, life-loving family. They were very dark skinned, part Dutch and part Malaysian.

Pappie worked for BAT on Java till 1957, which is when Dutch colonials were ordered out of the country. He was sent to Ghana, West Africa, where I joined him for some months after finishing school and before becoming an au pair in England.

Having set up a new plant and supervised the tobacco fields in Ghana for a few years, he went to work in Malaysia. He had become a director with BAT by then and travelled often to England.

He took early retirement and decided cold and grey Holland was no place for him to retire. My parents kept the house in Holland for spending the summers in, but Spain seemed a more suitable climate. Thus, together with many ex-colonials, My parents settled in a place in the mountains near Malaga, called El Atabal.

Eventually, having always enjoyed the luxury of a chauffeur, they found the laborious trips across Europe too much for them, and they decided to give up the house in Spain. Plane travel had not yet become either cheap or available the way it is now.

Retirement in Hollandsche Rading, near Hilversum, spelled the end for him. He had no hobbies, did not enjoy the Dutch way of life, missed the tropical food, and never settled or tried to enjoy living in cold, crowded, Holland.

He was a man of the tropics. He died at the very young age of 62. Although he very rarely referred to them, the war years had taken their toll.

WE THAT ARE LEFT TO GROW OLD WITH THE YEARS
REMEMBERING THE HEART ACHE, THE PAIN AND THE TEARS,
HOPING AND PRAYING THAT NEVER AGAIN
<MAN WILL SINK TO SUCH SORROW AND SHAME
THE PRICE THAT WAS PAID WE WILL ALWAYS REMEMBER,
EVERY DAY, EVERY MONTH, NOT JUST IN NOVEMBER
WE SHALL REMEMBER THEM

The Far Eastern POW prayer

Dates entered into the front page of my father's small bible, which he carried with him during his years of imprisonment by the Nippon. Not all entries are legible. I have translated the Dutch entries into English.

Niek Hoorn worked on the Burma railway before this appalling journey took place, and these entries tell of his journey from Burma to Japan. It seems the Japs took from April 1943 to August 1944 to move their prisoners of war to work in Japan.

The Americans dropped the bombs on Nagasaki and Hiroshima in August 1945, thereby ending the war.

24/4/43 Aankomst Tarso/Arrival Tarso
17/3/44 Aankomst Tamocan/Arrival Tamocan
22/6/44 vertrek naar Singapore/Leave for Singapore
22/6/44 Aankomst Singapore, Camp Rivers ... vml ... arg/Arrive Singapore, Camp Rivers
3/7/44 vertrek Singapore naar Japan /leave Singapore for Japan
16/7/44 Aankomst Manilla/Arrive at Manilla
25/7/44 de Jong dood, aankomst Jakao (Formosa)/de Jong dies, arrival at Jakao (Formosa)
1/8/44 Korve (Formosa)
10/8/44 Moedji, Japan
11/8/44 Aankomst Kamp Jokcaitor/Arrival at Camp Jocaitor
7/10/44 Overstroming/Floods
5/11/44 eerste luchtalarm/first air alarm
7/12/44 Aardbeving/Earthquake

1/6/45 Vertrek 300 m naar Tajama/Move 300 m to Tajama

18/6/45 eerste bommen op de fabriek 12 ... r ... t/First bomb on factory ...

6- ... ... 45 bombardement op fabriek, luchtalarm/bombardment on factory, air alarm

November 1944, 7x alarm

December 1944, 26x alarm

Januarie 1945, 47x alarm

Februarie 1945, 48x alarm

Maart 1945, 37x alarm

April 1945, 45x alarm

Mei 1945, 45x alarm

Juni 1945, 54x alarm

Hanneke Coates

THE FORGIVENESS PROJECT www.forgivenessproject.com

My father's war records

42a Buckingham Palace Road,

London SW1W 0RE, England, United Kingdom

I first learned about the Forgiveness Project from a story I read in the *Church Times*. It was about someone whose sister had been murdered by the notorious Englishman Dr Shipman. The story of forgiveness so inspired me and changed my life forever. I knew instantly it was what I had been searching for.

Those of us sharing our stories of forgiveness do so in the hope that we can inspire others who are struggling to make sense of life's cruelty and man's inhumanity to others. All our stories are different. Some of us who share our stories have a faith of one kind or another, while others do not. But we all share that sense of peace we've received through forgiveness.

Marina Cantacuzino inspired the birth of the Forgiveness Project and its exhibition. She came to see me, and she just listened. I am now one of Marina's storytellers. It is by sharing our stories that in our own small way each of us hopes to encourage people to start their pilgrimages of forgiveness.

The National Memorial Arboretum in Stafford is a Landscapes of Life Exhibition. Its organizers have given space and recognition to many large and small regiments as well as groups of people who were previously unrecognized by the nation but who contributed in their own unselfish ways during the two world wars. Space is given to those who fought with us and also those who fought against us.

A sleeper from the 'death railway' in Burma has been laid in the park to acknowledge that for every sleeper on the 258 miles hacked through the jungle one POW man died while building that railway line.

I would like to use these pages to encourage those who manage the park to acknowledge that army of faithful people in Japan, "the researchers." These people, in all humility, face the generations of often-bewildered and still-grieving people who lost members of their families on that fateful journey through the jungle or in the hundreds of POW camps in Japan or the Dutch East Indies archipelago.

It is this group of "researchers" that have been able to bring some sense of peace and closure to those of us who knew about their suffering yet did not know the details. Now we are able to fill in the gaps of the lost years while our loved ones were imprisoned. We now know where it was they were imprisoned or died and were buried or cremated.

As in most stories of forgiveness, it was that small group of people and to me the most unlikely people I could ever have dreamt of," the Japanese," who finally helped me break the last pieces of the shell that had enclosed my understanding.

I have finally learned to let go of the legacy of pain.